THE SWAN

SEBASTIANO VASSALLI was born in 1941. He took a degree in literature and has been a schoolteacher and a dealer in antiques. His solid reputation in Italy as a novelist has been confirmed with the award of the prestigious Strega prize to *The Chimera* which, like *The Swan*, has been published throughout Europe. He lives with his family near Novara.

EMMA ROSE won the John Florio prize with the first book she translated, Marta Morazzoni's novel *His Mother's House*.

By the same author in English

THE CHIMERA

Sebastiano Vassalli

THE SWAN

A novel

Translated from the Italian
by Emma Rose
With a Preface to this edition
by the Author

THE HARVILL PRESS
LONDON

First published in Italy with the title *Il Cigno*
by Giulio Einaudi editore, Milan, 1993

First published in Great Britain in 1997
by The Harvill Press,
84 Thornhill Road,
London N1 1RD

1 3 5 7 9 8 6 4 2

© Giulio Einaudi editore s.p.a., 1993
English translation © Emma Rose, 1997
Preface © Sebastiano Vassalli, 1997
Translation of preface © The Harvill Press, 1997

Sebastiano Vassalli asserts the moral right to be
identified as the author of this work

A CIP catalogue record for this book
is available from the British Library

ISBN 1 86046 299 5 (hbk)
ISBN 1 86046 300 2 (pbk)

Designed and typeset in Stempel Garamond at
Libanus Press, Marlborough, Wiltshire

Printed and bound in Great Britain by Butler & Tanner Ltd
at Selwood Printing, Burgess Hill

Contents

Author's Preface to the British Edition

It happens in every story about human beings: there is one moment, never to be repeated, in the fortunes of individuals as in those of nations, when the truth will out. For the city of Palermo and for the whole of Sicily, the moment of truth came in the summer of 1904, when the Sicilians accorded the most triumphal welcome home from exile to the protagonists of the first-ever Italian trial in which the word "mafia" was mentioned: two men had come to symbolise the islanders' pride, and they were almost certainly guilty of horrible crimes. For the first and only time in its history, an entire population came out and declared itself: it drew itself up in battle order, organised itself into a Pro Sicily Committee with branches even in America, demonstrated in the streets and squares of every town on the island, sent telegrams to the government in Rome and eventually obtained what it had set out to achieve. The men suspected of the murder of Marchese Emanuele Notarbartolo, men who had been found guilty at a first trial, were absolved "for lack of evidence", eleven years after the crime; the key witnesses were now dead or had retracted. They were borne home in triumph only to sink into oblivion within a matter of weeks: a sign that the Sicilians, in defending them, had meant above all to defend their island, and that indeed, in their way, they had judged the pair guilty. Giuseppe Fontana, the executioner, emigrated to America; Raffaele Palizzolo, who ordered the killing and had been an important politician, ended his days reciting poems to the Palermo street-arabs.

This story is a hundred years old, but it tells us all that needs to be understood, or nearly all, about the mafia: even about today's mafia. I confess I have been naïve enough to write it down as a service to my country: I hoped it would be possible for me, in relating the history of a people, to do what a psychoanalyst does with the history of his patients, helping them bring to light the deep-buried mechanisms of their neuroses. It never occurred to me that such an illness is the patient's normal condition; that patients cling to their own neuroses, and that my "therapeutic" book would end by unleashing – as very promptly happened – the same defence-mechanisms that had been triggered at the Palizzolo trial and after his condemnation.

Naturally the reactions to a book are of little account in comparison with the passions that can be aroused from news-stories. I am still alive and *The Swan* has had and continues to find many readers in every part of Italy, including Sicily. But a hatchet job has been done on me; techniques and methods of the mafia culture have been (and continue to be) deployed against me in an attack on two fronts in particular. The one is what one might call literary criticism, and here the word has been that my book lacks originality: it is a reportage knocked together out of all the commonplaces about the mafia that have been current in literature and the cinema for the last hundred years. On the plane of historical reconstruction, however, since the event is not subject to wholesale denial, an effort has been made – and will continue to be made – to find ways to undermine it bit by bit, tossing in false assertions which cost nothing to those who make them but which would oblige me, if I wanted to rebut them, to under-take a continual, exhausting and, above all, humiliating labour of correction . . . Finally, the most absurd argument has been invoked without restraint: not being a Sicilian by birth, I cannot have any grasp of the Sicilian situation. (It seems incredible, but that's how it is. On the eve of the year Two Thousand, apparently respectable people, who write for the papers and teach in the universities, come out with this sort of assertion.)

The love of the patient for his disease remains as strong as ever; and there would indeed be grounds for despair were there not other factors to permit a degree of optimism. For instance the realisation that a certain way of representing the mafia and the mafiosi – Leonardo Sciascia's *The Day of the Owl* is an example – is no longer practised today and would no longer even be possible. Italians have seen people like Totò Riina, Leoluca Bagarella and Giovanni Brusca on television, and have recognised that no obscure grandeur, no ancient wisdom subsists in these men. For the first time in centuries, the aura of legend and mystery that surrounds the "honoured society" has in part dissolved.

S.V.

5 December 1996

Hell (1893–1894)

I

From Sciara to Palermo, 1 February 1893

With a short blast of the whistle, a sharp jolt and a lingering groan of old metal beneath the passengers' feet, the stopping train to Palermo was on its way again, every joint of its ancient carriages squealing and creaking. From the distant locomotive came the sound of trapped steam wheezing in the boiler while the thud of the pistons became louder and faster as the train picked up speed. Alone in a first-class compartment, Commendator Emanuele Notarbartolo lifted one of the arm-rests which divided the red velour seats and stretched out almost to his full length. He felt tired but satisfied. This year, once again, he had managed to visit the family estate to supervise the work for the new season, as his father – God rest his soul – had always urged him to do. He had inspected the pruning and tasted the new wine; he had verified that the quantity and quality of seed matched the price paid for it; he had seen to the mending of the barrels and collected a small overdue rent payment . . .

With an upward glance he checked that the double-barrelled shotgun, from which he had removed the cartridges – a precaution he always took before boarding a train – was securely stowed in the luggage-rack. He tried to look outside to see where he was, but the window – streaked across with rain and almost opaque – enabled him to distinguish only the vague outlines of prickly-pears, dry-stone walls and cane thickets, which leapt out at him, then immediately disappeared into the dying light of a grey, wet day on the very brink of night. He pulled his silver watch from his waistcoat pocket. It was twenty past five and the *commendatore*, vexed, shook his head, thinking of his wife and daughter, who at that precise moment were probably leaving home to go and meet him at the station where he would arrive, at best, half an hour late . . .

"Can't they be on time even once?" he grumbled to himself. "Damn these trains!"

He sank back against the red pile of the seat, allowing his legs, arms and even his head to sway and bounce to the rhythm of the train in the half-light of the compartment. He gazed at the innumerable tiny raindrops on the window and the olive and citrus groves of the Torto valley beyond, but his thoughts were elsewhere – in Palermo, at the head office of the Bank of Sicily whose chairman he, Emanuele Notarbartolo, had been for thirteen years; the bank he had had to leave in 1890, when the then Prime Minister Francesco Crispi and his Sicilian friends had forced him out . . . A conspiracy to defraud, that's what it was! They were simply a gang of thieves, great and small; as soon as he left, they had thrown themselves into gambling on the stock exchange with the Bank's money, drawing out vast sums in the name of people who'd been dead for years and generally embezzling in every conceivable way, without even bothering to camouflage the discrepancies in the books. This plundering, reflected the *commendatore*, had been going on for more than two years now, and they were still at it; but ever since the change of government in Rome, honest people throughout the whole of Italy, even Palermo, had once more begun to hope that they might recover the posts they had been ousted from, and be able to restore order in all areas of the public administration. The new Prime Minister, the Marchese di Rudiní, had informed Notarbartolo that he was counting on him to drive the thieves out of the Bank of Sicily, and the *commendatore*, who asked for nothing better, had already succeeded in catching one of them red-handed and denouncing him to the appropriate authorities. The incident had occurred two months previously, at the end of November. The Honourable Raffaele Palizzolo, a Member of Parliament who sat on the Bank's board, having played the stock market with the savers' money, made the mistake of crediting the winnings in his own name, instead of to some front man or company. The cheque was even now sitting on the Prime Minister's desk in Rome.

The train juddered over some points. As they neared Cerda station to the piercing squeal of brake blocks tightening around wheels, houses came into view on the other side of the road and the platforms appeared, glistening with rain and bearing the dark shapes of travellers sheltering beneath their hoods or umbrellas. Finally the train ground to a halt in a cloud of pure white steam and Commendator Notarbartolo, still looking out of his window, had the opportunity to witness a small incident which surprised him and aroused his curiosity. A tall, bearded man with glasses approached his compartment with one hand raised to open the door, and would certainly have done so, had a railwayman on the platform not waved him to the next compartment, adding a few words which Notarbartolo could not make out for the deafening noise of the engine.

Insignificant though it was, the scene unsettled him. "Since when," he asked himself, "have railway inspectors had the authority to choose a passenger's compartment? Surely once you've bought your ticket you sit where you like!"

But just then the train moved off again with its usual cacophony of slamming doors and old iron under intolerable strain. Commendator Notarbartolo dismissed the question with a shrug, muttering under his breath:

"So much the better! He's saved me the bother of making conversation with a stranger." When the inspector came by to check the tickets he might ask – just out of curiosity – who the man with the glasses was, and why he'd been advised to move on when he already had his foot on the step of Notarbartolo's compartment . . .

The train was running beside the sea now, and the certainty of that presence in the winter evening soothed the thoughts of our first-class passenger and brought them back into harmony with the panting of the engine and the bluish light which he himself had switched on inside the carriage. He leant his forehead against the window. There it was, the sea, leaden grey and empty of sails, but for one moment Notarbartolo saw the scene as it was in the summer, when the sun kindled gleams of gold on the sand and the water between the rocks teemed with life, as on the day the world was made . . . This was the country of his childhood, the place he hoped to retire to in a few years' time – once all his daughters, down to the very youngest, were married, and once Palermo and the Bank of Sicily were safely in the hands of honest and capable managers. That time was still a long way off, however, and the *commendatore*'s thoughts returned to the Bank's head offices in Palermo, where things of such gravity were happening that they made market speculation and loans to the dead look like child's play. For the past month – perhaps even two – the mint of the Bank of Sicily had been used, unbeknown to everybody, to print banknotes with serial numbers already in circulation: counterfeit money! And those notes which should never have existed, those cursed notes which brought hunger, misery and emigration to the poor, were being used by the political masters up in Rome to pay off the hundreds of thousands of lire bills for their own electoral campaigns and those of their friends – those same bills which lately had been creating shame and scandal in the Bank of Rome, making the headlines in all the papers, and which had already caused arrests and suicides . . . Now that the scandal had finally erupted, someone or other in Palermo was busy trying to cover it all up and pay everybody off with the Bank of

Sicily's forged notes. But he, Notarbartolo, wouldn't let them get away with it.

He straightened in his seat again and, looking out at the darkness beyond the window, saw the reflection of a man he did not immediately recognise: a man with a frown, threatening eyes and a deep furrow running down the middle of his forehead.

"Am I really that ugly when I get angry?" he asked himself. Immediately his wrinkles disappeared and the reflected face shifted and rearranged itself into the suggestion of a smile – Commendator Notarbartolo had just remembered what his son Leopoldo used to say when he was scolded as a child: "Don't get angry Daddy, you'll go all ugly!" He passed a hand over his unshaven cheek and, like the good Sicilian he was, concluded that those are the only things which really matter in life: one's family, one's children . . .

So gradually that it almost escaped his notice, the darkness outside the window had begun to fill with lights, and the interior of the train to echo with noises. A voice had called out from carriage to carriage: "Termini Imerese! Termini Imerese!" Then there appeared the station lamps, the tin canopy over the platforms; the advertisements for Kalodont toothpaste ("a world-class product") and for Bertelli throat-pastilles (with its picture of an eagle clasping a box in its talons). The train usually stopped for at least twenty minutes at Termini, because the railwaymen had to couple the two trains bound for Palermo: one coming from Catania and one from Messina. Along the platform, food-sellers offered their wares with long, rhythmic cries like lamentations:

"Lemon water", "Salt lupins", "Hot chick-pea fritters" . . .

Commendator Notarbartolo took a few steps in the compartment to stretch his legs. He looked out onto the platform and was surprised to see the same inspector who had redirected the bespectacled traveller at Cerda. He was standing there with a signal-lamp in his hand, rather as if he were mounting guard to the first-class carriage. Notarbartolo lowered the window and called out:

"Hey! You there!"

The inspector turned round. He was a short, thin man of about thirty-five, with a narrow moustache and a half-sinister, half-surprised expression, like someone who has been caught in the act. He looked at the person who had called him, then glanced over his shoulder towards the station, to make sure that the passenger wasn't talking to someone else.

"How late are we going to be getting in to Palermo?" inquired Notarbartolo.

The man in uniform looked scared. He fished his watch out of his pocket then stared at it for a long while, as if having difficulty telling the time.

"We'll be leaving in ten minutes," he finally said, without looking the recipient of this information in the eye. "We should be in Palermo around seven."

The *commendatore* would have liked to ask about the fellow who boarded the train in Cerda, but a whistle sounded from the engine which was attaching the carriages from Messina, and the whole train lurched forward a few yards. From beneath the station canopy, someone – perhaps a porter – began to sing a song that rose above the wheezing of the locomotive and other station sounds. The words were:

"Love, love, love
Love is bitter!
Love is like a cucumber:
One tip sweet and the other tip sour."

From the other side of the station, where a goods train was standing motionless in the dark, another equally tuneful voice replied:

"Love, love, love
Love is fire!
Love is like a furnace:
Try to blow it out and it burns higher."

Notarbartolo shut the window and returned to his seat.

"I wonder," he found himself thinking, "if there is any other country in the world where men sing like that, for no apparent reason, like birds – simply to give voice to their feelings?" And he thought how "his" Sicily was an earthly paradise, where people could have lived happily had it not been for a horribly venomous snake which lurked somewhere among the mint and the sage: the same serpent, perhaps, which tempted our progenitors in the Book of Genesis . . . He glanced at his watch again. He was beginning to weary of this journey. What was stopping the stationmaster from blowing his whistle, now that the coaches from Messina had been coupled to the train? Why not at least attempt to make up a little of the lost time? Through the window he saw that the ticket inspector was still there, beneath the canopy, talking to a brakeman who wore a railwayman's blue cap and a large handlebar moustache. The brakeman was pointing in the direction of the waiting rooms, and the inspector, judging by his gestures, was urging him to have patience: they would have to wait . . . Then they both turned towards the first-class carriage and only when they realized that they, in their turn, were observed, did they pretend to be watching the men from the Post Office, who happened to be passing at that moment. What was going on? A sudden, acute sense of danger flashed like lightning through Notarbartolo's mind. But there was no danger anywhere – only the rhythmical calls of the vendors, the monotonous rain, the advertisements, the gas-lamps . . .

When the bell began to ring announcing the departure of the train, the stationmaster came out of his office beneath the canopy and walked towards the engine. Puffing as heavily as

9

usual, the train moved off. From the first-class waiting room there emerged two men in dark suits, with stiff hats pulled down over their ears, and Notarbartolo realized that these were his assassins. He stared at them, his eyes dilated with terror, as they advanced towards the moving train at a brisk pace, but not running. He saw the guard direct them to a compartment – his compartment. He saw the door open and the two men enter the blue light. One of them – the fatter man with the face scarred by smallpox – threw himself down on the seat opposite and eyed Notarbartolo as if assessing how much resistance he would put up when having his throat cut. The other – the one with the wide face and the deep-set eyes – shut the door, turned his back on Notarbartolo and stood in front of the window while the train clattered over the tangle of glistening wet points and left behind the last of the station's gas-lamps, heading for the darkness of the open countryside at night, with no hope of return . . .

Notarbartolo was alone and desperate, as every man is alone and desperate in the face of death. Shouting would be futile, because even if the other passengers had heard him, they wouldn't have been able to come to his aid: the carriage was made up of three large compartments, cut off one from the other and only accessible from the outside. If his shotgun had not been empty, he thought, this last encounter with destiny would not have been so unequal! But the weapon lay quite harmless up there in the rack and he had neither the time nor the means to load it. His only hope was to try to seize it by the barrel and use it as a club . . .

The engine had picked up speed. Immediately after the bridge over the San Leonardo river there is a tunnel which the Palermo train hurtled into, whistling like a fiend and filling the enclosed space with steam. At that moment the man who had been standing at the window turned round and signalled to his companion, who produced from his jacket a bread knife with an eight-inch serrated blade.

Notarbartolo flung himself towards the gun in the rack. The movement probably cost him his life, because the first blow sliced into his abdomen while he still had both arms above his head. He clutched at the rack, which broke, and he fell forwards. With a strength born of despair he tried to reach the door and throw himself out, but they held him back by the arms and forced him to stand, while his screams were drowned in the roar of the train charging through the tunnel and the man with the scarred face kept sinking the knife into him and pulling it out again under the blue light of the compartment. As in a dream, Notarbartolo watched the blood-stained knife emerge from his body at least three times, then the compartment, the train and the whole world seemed flooded by an explosion of light. His legs buckled, his eyes rolled upwards and he saw no more. He lay jammed between the seats, jerking and scratching marks into the pile of the seats with his fingernails, still desperately attempting to cling to life.

At this point the other man, who until then had done no more than help the murderer by restraining the victim, pulled a claspknife from his jacket pocket, opened it and stabbed the dying man in the back three times, aiming for his heart. He pulled him up and, with one last blow that had blood spraying everywhere, cut his throat. Only when he was absolutely certain that no trace of life remained in the body which lay before him, did Don Piddu *Facci di lignu* (Woodenface), for such was the nickname of that ferocious individual, clean his bloodied hand on his victim's jacket, then close the claspknife and replace the weapon in his pocket.

As the train emerged from the tunnel it slowed down to negotiate the points leading in to the station of Trabia. Don Piddu gestured to the pock-marked man and they lifted the body into a sitting position in one corner of the seat, and covered Commendator Notarbartolo with his own coat as if he were sleeping. Then Don Piddu positioned himself in front of the door, in case any incautious passenger should take it into his head to make for that particular compartment. But when the train drew to a halt, the only people to be seen on the glistening, rain-soaked platform were the stationmaster and the inspector, the latter of whom called out: "Trabia! Trabia!" then walked past the first-class carriage and gave Don Piddu a look that said: "Did everything go to plan? Is he dead?"

Almost imperceptibly, Don Piddu lowered his eyelids in assent, and the railwayman clenched his left fist and raised the thumb in a victory sign: "We did it!"

Once again the engine whistled and the train moved off. *Facci di lignu* stepped away from the window while, inside the compartment, his assistant asked:

"What do we do now, Don Piddu?"

Without moving a muscle in his face, Don Piddu leant over the dead man. He removed a small gold cross from around his neck, pulled his wallet out of his inside jacket pocket and took his watch, breaking the fine silver chain so as to make the motive of robbery seem all the more likely. Then he looked pityingly at the man who had spoken: a certain Peppi Lauriano, a ruffian – a *malacarne* – who, with this murder of so important a figure, had signed his own death warrant, but was too stupid even to realize it. He replied in dialect, with an old saying still used nowadays when people ask foolish questions:

"We'll do what the ancients did – took out their stomachs and put in their navels."

Don Piddu went over to the door and opened it with some caution, because the train reached its top speed between stations and he could have been shaken out. A gust of steam and rain filled the compartment, but *Facci di lignu* was unperturbed. He signalled to his companion to join him and do everything he did. The two dark-clad men took the corpse by the arms, lifted it and dragged it upright to the door, while the train, tearing through the night, streaked by a lighted level-crossing where a woman wearing a railway cap lifted both hands to her face in the act of screaming. They gave the corpse a shove – or, to be more exact, Don Piddu gave it a shove – and sent it rolling down the short railway embankment as the lights of Altavilla were appearing in the distance.

When he had finally succeeded in closing the compartment door, Don Piddu swore at Peppi Lauriano:

"*Chi mi stocchi!* (Damn and blast you! or words to that effect). What the hell came over you? You left me to do it all on my own, and we're nearly at the station!"

But Lauriano was afraid. "That woman . . ." he stammered. "The woman at the level-crossing . . . She saw the body. She saw us push it off the train! We've got to go back and kill her!"

Facci di lignu bent over to pick up the dead man's gun, which had rolled under the seat in the struggle. He straightened his hat and got ready to leave the train, examining his reflection in the same window in which his victim had seen himself an hour earlier.

"That woman," Don Piddu replied calmly, "saw nothing."

2

Villabate, 1 April 1893

Sergio Trabia had generous globs of sauce on his chin, his cheeks and his forehead. He lifted a hand that looked like a bunch of bananas and, without specifically addressing his host – the Honourable Raffaele Palizzolo – or any of his fellow-guests, let drop a question which astonished everybody.

"What if we've killed him for nothing?" he asked.

Instantly a deep silence fell and everyone at the table – even those who, seconds earlier, had been laughing and chatting with their neighbours – turned their eyes on the man who had spoken. From the way they were looking at him, Don Sergio concluded that he had committed something of a *faux pas* and that, if he didn't explain himself at once, his doubt would be mistaken for cowardice or – worse – infamy. He shrugged his shoulders.

"I don't know the first thing about banks," he said in his own defence, "but my impression is that we've got all we can out of the Bank of Sicily: the party's over. For a start, if today's papers are right and there's going to be a Central State Bank set up in Rome, they'll be printing the money there . . ."

"What do you mean, we killed him for nothing?" interrupted Don Antonio Perez Rizzuto. His expression and tone of voice alarmed the Honourable Palizzolo, because it was common knowledge that Perez Rizzuto and Trabia didn't get on, and the host's main concern during these gatherings was precisely to avoid arguments between his guests.

"Notarbartolo," Don Antonio articulated crisply, "was a worthless louse; he'd been troublesome before and looked like becoming even more so. His rotten life had to be stamped out. As for the rest, that's just gossip . . ."

"Newspapers print bollocks," opined another of the gallant men, or "lions" – *liuni* – who were gathered around the Honourable Palizzolo's table that day. He stood up. "Me, I'm illigiterate (illiterate)," he said. "I keep the newspapers in the bog and read them with my arse, but I've never found a piece of news that was any use." He bent over and passed a hand over his backside, as if wiping himself. "That," he announced, "is how I read the papers."

The room burst into raucous laughter: "Ha, ha, ha! He reads them with his arse!" and the Honourable Palizzolo, who had been ready to intervene to keep the peace, leant back in his chair and looked round with legitimate pride at his guests, all now laughing riotously and slapping each other on the back like any harmless group of friends larking about. No other Sicilian politician, he thought to himself, could gather under his roof as many Heads of Families and Men of Honour as were sitting round his table that evening. He passed them in review. Starting from the right, the first of the *liuni* was Don Piddu *Facci di lignu* who, in court and police documents, was referred to as "Giuseppe Fontana, son of the late Vincenzo", to distinguish him from another multiple murderer known as "Giuseppe Fontana, son of the late Rosario". Like his namesake, whenever the police managed to get him into court on charges such as "robbery", "robbery with violence", "murder", or "criminal conspiracy", he always ended up being acquitted for lack of evidence.

Next to Don Piddu sat the head of the Altavilla Family, Sergio Trabia, who, having aired his doubts on the usefulness of Notarbartolo's death, had now returned his attention to his plate and was wolfing down his food, emitting a steady noise rather like that of a suction pump. Next came the heads of the Monreale Family, Don Francesco Vitale and Don Nicolò Trapani, recently risen to fame in the newspapers for the murder of a certain Francesco Miceli, who had dared to compete with the Honourable Palizzolo for the purchase of the estate of the aristocratic Gentile family. Before surrendering his soul to God, poor Miceli managed to give the police the names of his assassins, but even that final effort proved useless: the inquiry was terminated because of the usual lack of evidence, and the two gentlemen regained their liberty. Then there was Filippo Pesco, known as *lu Gaddu* (The Cockerel), who controlled all the prostitutes and small pimps in Palermo. His friends swore that he owed his nickname to those remarkable amatory powers which, in his youth, had enabled him to seduce dozens of women and personally initiate them into prostitution. Next to him sat the heads of the city Families: Andrea Saccone of the Albergaria district (Palizzolo's constituency); Antonio Perez Rizzuto of the Capo district, where Palizzolo lived, and Filippo Giamporcaro of Fieravecchia. (The last, in particular, was famous for having killed his predecessor and eaten his heart, as well as for scores of other murders.) Then came the men who procured Palizzolo his votes and business deals: Don Raffaele's brother, Eugenio Palizzolo, who acted as his front; Luciano Ania, town councillor and president of the Chamber of Commerce, and Salvatore Anfossi, financier and stockbroker. And lastly, to the host's left sat his *curatolo* Matteo Filippello – steward of the Villabate estate where the Honourable Member's *liuni* occasionally convened for lunch or dinner, and where today's gathering was also taking place.

Salvatore Anfossi, financial expert and treasurer for the Palizzolo clan, addressed his companions:

"I don't believe Italy is likely to get a central bank like England or France in the near future," he said. "There will be a transitional stage and the Bank of Sicily will stay autonomous for another five or ten years. So a rat like Notarbartolo, if he'd lived, could have caused us a lot of trouble. He'd have carried on sticking his nose into our affairs and sooner or later he'd have managed to whip up a scandal."

"In Parliament all the Sicilian members, except perhaps the Socialists, will defend the autonomy of the Bank of Sicily," said Palizzolo. "So will His Excellency Francesco Crispi, who's using our money to pay his bills up there in Rome . . . As for the newspapers," he added after a brief pause, "I wouldn't attach too much importance to the fuss they've been making lately over thieving politicians and the need to reform the banking system. The newspapers sway the opinions and passions of the general public like the wind blows dust, but no man worthy of respect has ever stopped looking after his own interests because of other people's opinions. No man has ever abandoned his chosen path because he met a little wind and dust along the way . . ."

After these poetical excursions into the realms of wind, dust and other people's opinions, the conversation fragmented again. There was a small mishap – the breaking of a saltcellar – which was generally considered unlucky and provoked many exclamations and vulgar gestures and much swearing at the culprit. Sergio Trabia kept his face buried in his plate, lifting it only occasionally to wipe himself from forehead to chin, or to laugh with his mouth full when someone near him said something he considered amusing. They spoke of whores, as they always did when Filippo Pesco was present. They spoke of old friends who had emigrated to America. But above all they spoke of the investigation into the death of Commendator Notarbartolo. Favourable comments were made about the police, who on this occasion had proved to be even more inept and muddle-headed than usual. In the days immediately following the crime they had arrested signalmen, passers-by, railwaymen and other unfortunates who eventually had to be released for lack of evidence. After two months of haphazard investigation and futile arrests, the only person still in prison was Giuseppe Carollo – the ticket inspector who, at Termini Imerese station, had shown Don Piddu and his assistant the victim's compartment, and later on, at Trabia, had returned to make sure the mission had been accomplished.

"Carollo is in serious trouble," said Don Nicolò Trapani. "Now that the investigation has been halted and there are no other suspects, he runs the risk of being used as a scapegoat, to bring the whole business to an end. The authorities in Rome and Palermo, public opinion, the press – they all want somebody to get life. If the police and magistrates can't come up with a more convincing murderer it's possible – it's more than likely – that that somebody will be him."

"Is there any risk he'll talk? What does he know?" Don Luciano Ania asked.

Don Piddu glanced at the local councillor with the impassive expression which had earned him the nickname *Facci di lignu*, and said, or to be more exact, passed sentence:

"For the time being Carollo isn't talking. If he shows any sign of squealing in future, we'll silence him."

The Honourable Palizzolo frowned and asked:

"How much money did Carollo get? What are his family circumstances?"

It transpired from the embarrassed replies of Salvatore Anfossi, Andrea Saccone and Don Piddu himself that so far Giuseppe Carollo had received only one thousand lire, which he'd had to share with a certain Francesco Comella, waiting-room attendant at Termini Imerese, and one Pancrazio Garufi, the brakeman on the train when Notarbartolo had been bumped off. Not much for someone who had already been in prison for two months, and ran the risk of getting a life sentence. What is more, the railwayman had a wife and four small children. The wife had already started talking more than was safe, putting it about that her husband was in prison to cover for someone else . . . Don Raffaele pulled a face.

"We must provide for this woman at once," he said to Salvatore Anfossi. "Give her some money to keep her going until the trial. Two or three thousand lire – you decide. After the trial we'll see what's best, but in the meantime Carollo must stay calm and mustn't have to worry about his family – otherwise he really might talk." He also suggested giving five hundred lire to Margherita Romano, the level-crossing keeper who had seen Notarbartolo's body being thrown from the train, to reward her discretion under interrogation.

"Carollo won't talk," Andrea Saccone said, "not even if he gets life. I'll vouch for that. He's a man of honour like his father Santo and his grandfather Carmelo."

"And Peppi Lauriano?" Filippo Pesco asked. "My women down at the port haven't seen or heard of him since. What's happened to him?"

Peppi Lauriano was the man with the scarred face, the *malacarne* who had assisted Don Piddu in his business on the train. Nobody had come across him since and many faces turned to *Facci di lignu*, but he remained impassive. Matteo Filippello spoke up instead.

"Peppi Lauriano," he said, "came to hide in my house, as we'd arranged. He was feeling a bit off-colour, so I put some medicine in his coffee to make him better."

At the mention of medicine and coffee, many of the guests started chuckling. One or two feigned concern:

"Where was it hurting? His head? His stomach? His prick?"

Matteo Filippello shook his head.

"No, no, he wasn't in any pain," he told them with a straight face. "He hadn't even noticed, poor man, but he'd started sprouting the horns of treachery . . . He's much better now."

The laughter which followed these words was so loud and

riotous that it made the window panes tremble and the plates rattle on the table that had been laid with silver cutlery and embroidered tablecloths – all property of the estate's previous owners. Those of the *liuni* who had allowed themselves to be overcome by laughter as they ate even began to choke, and their neighbours had to come to their rescue by slapping and punching them on the back hard enough to leave bruises for a month. Finally, when all the guests had more or less regained their composure, a voice at the end of the table said scornfully: "*Carnazza!*" – (good riddance). And this, a few weeks after his demise, was the commemorative speech for Giuseppe "Peppi" Lauriano, poisoned because his friends did not think they could trust him and because, in any case, he was of no more use to them.

By the end of dinner all Don Raffaele's guests were in high spirits, induced both by the wine and by that sort of inebriation which eating and joking in company can engender in those accustomed to regarding the world as composed exclusively of enemies. Even Don Piddu *Facci di lignu* laughed, as dogs laugh, lifting his upper lip to reveal two steel teeth: canines which one of his many victims had managed to smash in before he died. Sergio Trabia unleashed a burp loud enough to bring a blush to the faces of the painted Cupids at the four corners of the ceiling, but nobody took any notice, so he loosened his tie and unbuttoned his collar in order to be more comfortable in case of a repetition. Almost all the guests were smoking fat cigars from a box which Don Raffaele had passed round after he had taken one himself and got Matteo Filippello to light it for him. Salvatore Anfossi, sitting across the table from Don Francesco Vitale, was telling him about the extraordinary opportunities for enrichment available to those who emigrated to the United States of America and how, if speculating with money from the Bank of Sicily ever became impossible, he planned to cross the ocean himself. Filippo Giamporcaro and Nicolò Trapani were exchanging whispered confidences about a young whore they both knew.

When a voice called out: "What are we waiting for? It's time for the toasts!" Don Raffaele rang the bell to summon the servants with the champagne. Everybody touched glasses and announced a toast to something: to business, to whores, to the health of friends and the death of enemies, to the knife which had taken Notarbartolo from this world, to Don Raffaele . . .

"Don Raffaele!" clamoured his *liuni* from various parts of the table. "A speech, Don Raffaele!"

The Honourable Palizzolo rose to his feet, glass in hand. He was a small, rotund man, so short that, as he stood up, his head was no higher than those of some of the *liuni* seated at his table. He had the round face of an ageing baby, with a rather sparse handlebar moustache, and he was wearing a bow tie, a colourful waistcoat and a velvet frock coat that reached down almost to his knees. Before relinquishing his champagne glass he raised it in the direction of Don Piddu Fontana, who was sitting to his right.

"Let us honour Don Piddu," he said, "and the generous Villabate family, who helped him and made his mission possible! The enemy they rid us of was a man who did not deserve to live. I'll go further: a villain who was plotting our ruin, but only succeeded in ruining himself. We, who acted in defence of our families, our honour, our sacred business interests, are not to blame for his death. Our hands are clean, our consciences spotless . . ."

As he spoke, Don Raffaele's arms and eyes and indeed his every feature were in constant motion, while he pitched his voice in a way that, ever since boyhood, had earned him the nickname of *Cignu* (The Swan). Whatever the subject, were it sardine fishing or the future of the human race, he would launch into it like an actor reciting some long, tragic monologue, or a poet aflame with the sacred fire of inspiration, improvising verses for an audience. Sergio Trabia removed a toothpick from the corner of his mouth, leant towards Francesco Vitale and growled admiringly:

"What a talker! Not even a priest at the altar talks like that!"

Don Francesco nodded in agreement: "*Parla comu un Ciciruni*" (He talks like a Cicero).

"The enemy is dead," The Swan continued, warming to his subject, "and we rejoice, because our enemies' death is our life. As the ancient Romans said: *mors tua, vita mea*. But we are not so heartless as to toast the death of a fellow human being, however odious his memory and however numerous our reasons for wanting to be rid of him. Let us instead drink a toast to our honour, which scum like Notarbartolo will never tarnish, and to the friendship which unites us and is our strength!" He threw his head back and flapped his arms like a swan about to take flight.

"Honour," he declaimed, gazing out over the heads of his guests, "is what makes us men. A man without honour is a man who does not exist. He has no friends, he is not respected, he cannot count on his family or even on himself. He is not a man. He is a pebble in the middle of the road, trodden on by every passer-by; he is a urinal in the corner of a square, pissed on by all and sundry . . ."

While The Swan, drunk with his own voice, was floating high on the wings of eloquence, something happened which neither he nor his guests heeded. We, however, must concern ourselves with it, both because it introduces a new character to our story and because it reveals an important facet of our protagonist's personality. A tall, thin woman in black appeared in the doorway and stood listening to the orator, gazing at him with affection of an intensity usually encountered only in the canine world. This woman, named Matilde, was The Swan's second cousin but, more importantly, had been his intended – his *zita* – for the past thirty-four years; ever since the distant spring of

1860 when (his baby-face still hairless) he used to rant about following Garibaldi to the ends of the earth and making Italy into one nation . . . In those days, The Swan was convinced that his future lay in literature. He even wrote a novel entitled *Elvira Trezzi*, which was serialised in the *Giornale di Sicilia*. Subsequently he immersed himself in politics and his life and appearance changed, but even then he and Matilde did not marry, because – as Don Raffaele would explain to those who inquired about the delay – the fact that they were blood-relatives prevented it. In such cases a special permit was needed from the church authorities and it wasn't easy to come by.

This matter of a permit had gone on for decades and was still unresolved at the time of our story. In the Palizzolo household it was taken as read that, as soon as the licence was finally granted, the two love-birds would fly to the altar. But nobody believed this any more, not even Matilde who, despite having a house of her own in Palermo, lived permanently in The Swan's home, sharing an apartment with his unmarried sisters and treating him like a brother. Those who knew her denied that her relationship with Don Raffaele had ever been anything other than spiritual – an infinite affection and devotion towards a man who, in her eyes, was little less than a god. She was less a fiancée or a wife than a votary, prepared to lay down her life for the superior being to whom she had consecrated her entire existence. The Swan, who could hardly fail to be moved by such loyalty, repaid her with an occasional indulgent glance, ironic remark or sometimes even a pat on her arm or a stroke of her hair. Matilde's joy at such times was so great that nothing in the world would have persuaded her to exchange it for the normal conjugal life of those among her acquaintances who despised her for being unmarried. She, alone among women, had the privilege of being The Swan's *zita* – what more could she ask of Fate? What more could she want from life?

After the toast had been drunk and The Swan had sat down

to the applause and cries of approval of the *liuni*, Matilde moved as if obeying a sudden impulse. She went up to her lord and master who, in the meantime, had raised a glass of champagne to his lips, and embraced and kissed him with such force that she made him choke and splutter:

"Stop it, stop it . . . you've made my champagne go down the wrong way . . . Give over, please!"

"You're the best!" she whispered in his ear. "Nobody in the whole world can talk like you!"

3

Palermo, 8 September 1893

His Excellency's Palermo flat was on the first floor of the Hotel Trinacria, opposite the Marina. The entrance was guarded by two plainclothes policemen who motioned the Honourable Member to stop. A stout, balding man arrived and, upon seeing The Swan, exclaimed: "Don Raffaele!"

"It's been too long, Don Peppino!" The Swan said, after they had embraced and kissed on both cheeks.

"You're the one who never visits us when you're up in Rome, Don Raffaele!" the other man reproved him. "Sometimes even His Excellency asks after you. 'Have you seen Palizzolo?' he says. 'Is he in Rome?'"

"What mood is His Excellency in today?" The Swan asked.

Giuseppe Palumbo Cardella ("Don Peppino") was Francesco Crispi's private secretary and knew the Honourable Palizzolo well, because they had been on the Bank of Sicily's board of directors together in the days when Notarbartolo still held sway and Crispi's men were outnumbered. He winked at Don Raffaele:

"His Excellency has been in splendid spirits lately," he replied, "but I wouldn't like you to be the one who goes and spoils them by talking about the Bank . . ."

The Swan raised his eyebrows and opened his arms wide.

"What else should I talk about, Don Peppino? World affairs? Everyone knows that's all His Excellency thinks about nowadays – international politics, Germany, France, the crisis in the

Balkans ... But our friends in Palermo couldn't give a toss about world politics! You know them as well as I do – they're worried about their business interests in the Bank of Sicily and they expect His Excellency to help them. If he doesn't, who will?"

"I'll go and find out if he'll see you," said Don Peppino.

At the time of our story the Honourable Francesco Crispi was a man of seventy-four, smaller and slighter in the flesh than he appeared in the photographs and drawings of illustrated weekly magazines. Seen close up, even the great drooping moustache wasn't as large or as thick as you would have expected. What was not apparent in the newspaper pictures, however, was his liveliness of expression and authoritative manner, which commanded the respect of all who met him. When The Swan entered his study, Francesco Crispi did him the honour of addressing him as "dear" ("My dear Palizzolo!"), but did not advance to greet him – even though he was already standing up – or hold out his hand. He had only just got back to the hotel after defending a client in court, and had removed collar and cuffs as well as his jacket and tie. The Swan, who was not used to meeting him in private, wondered whether to embrace and kiss him as he did at electoral banquets, or simply shake his hand. Wisely he went for the second option and found himself holding two of His Excellency's fingers, which were immediately withdrawn.

"You look wonderfully well, sir!" The Swan said. "In fine fettle!" He took a step back to get a better view of His Excellency's fettle. "The *Giornale di Sicilia* was quite right!" he exclaimed. "You look twenty years younger. Now that the whole of Italy – from the Alps to the southernmost tip of Sicily – is on your side, you've decided to prove that you're the most youthful and energetic of her politicians, not just by the freshness of your ideas, but by the very vigour of your physique!"

His Excellency acknowledged the compliment with a nod. He motioned his guest into an armchair and sat down opposite him, crossing his legs and resting both hands on his knee, as was his habit. What Palizzolo had said about his physique was true, and was a direct consequence of his political success: nothing in the world improved His Excellency's health like political success. During the riots and demonstrations which had swept cities and towns throughout Italy in reaction to the massacre of Italian miners at Aigues-Mortes, Crispi had been invoked as a saviour. Day by day a new party was taking shape in Parliament, in the newspapers and even in Court, made up of people from every social class and political tendency; people who wanted the return to power of the one man they considered capable of maintaining order internally and winning respect for Italy abroad – that man, of course, being His Excellency. In those last summer days of 1893, the popularity and success of Francesco Crispi was so great that even he appeared somewhat intimidated. He remained hidden away in his beloved Palermo, postponing week by week his expected return to the capital. The papers said he was behaving like a primadonna or a tenor who seeks to heighten an audience's anticipation by lingering in the wings before coming out to acknowledge their applause . . .

"Well, my dear Palizzolo," His Excellency repeated, "here we are. Can I help you in any way? – Either you personally, or our friends in Palermo?"

"First of all, Your Excellency," The Swan began, "allow me as a Member of Parliament to express the enthusiasm and hopes of the people of Palermo, who acclaim you, gather round you and entreat you to save Italy! Palermo and Sicily want Francesco Crispi to head the Government once more. And this popular desire which has manifested itself and continues to do so, even in the smallest, most remote villages of our island, is fervently shared by this speaker and by all Sicilian members of our nation's Parliament – with the sole exception, I believe, of the Socialists . . ."

His Excellency gave a start, and held up his palms as if to stem the flow of words. "The Socialists are the least of my problems!" he retorted. "Particularly in Sicily . . . My worst enemies are right here on this island, where the general public does indeed love me, as you just said. They're the landed gentry, the very people who used to say they'd do anything I asked. Now they want me dead . . . I'm not exaggerating." He raised a hand. "If there should be an attempt on my life," he said gravely, "it may be an anarchist who carries it out, but the large families of the Sicilian aristocracy will be behind it. However, I don't think Rudiní and the others will have me killed: that would require a courage they don't possess. All the Sicilian senators loathe me, from that worm Bordonar (who'd betray Our Lord Jesus Christ if he had the chance) to that degenerate Camporeale (so similar in body and soul to Verdi's Rigoletto) . . . In Parliament the Socialists are hostile, but at least they attack me openly, which is more than I can say for some deputies who owe their seats to me and claim they belong to my party while they plot and scheme against me with my enemies, thinking I don't know what they're up to . . . But such is human gratitude, and I'd be a fool to complain about it." He stopped, and looked Palizzolo in the eye.

"But enough of that sort of talk," he said, smiling. "Heaven knows where that would lead us. Let's get back to us . . . What did you come to talk about?"

As he listened to His Excellency's thoughts about those who wanted him dead and who might arm an assassin, The Swan remembered reading in some article that Francesco Crispi always kept a revolver within reach. He wondered where it might be at that moment: in his clothes? In a drawer? But the great man's waistcoat and trousers showed no sign of hiding any largish, heavy object, and none of the furniture in the room had drawers.

"Perhaps he keeps it under a cushion on his armchair, or in his bedroom . . ." he thought to himself. Neither could he see any trace of His Excellency's other secret weapon, the famous horn-shaped coral amulet which he kept with him to ward off evil influences. From time to time he would even take it out in Parliament – it could often be found in his hand when Nicotera or Guarnieri stood up to speak . . . People close to His Excellency maintained that a foolproof way to make him reach for his amulet was to mention the name of De Felice Giuffrida, a Socialist member from Catania, who incited Socialists in local government throughout Sicily against Crispi, and two years ago had even had the gall to seduce his wife. Every time His Excellency heard that name – said those in the know – he would scowl, mutter: *"Stu Cagliostru'n galera avi a muriri"* (That Cagliostro must end his days in prison), and feel for the coral horn in the same waistcoat pocket where possibly – or almost certainly – it lay at this very moment . . . However, when His Excellency suddenly asked: "What did you come to talk about?" The Swan's every thought focused once more on the Bank of Sicily – his reason for being there in the first place. He broached the subject in a roundabout way:

"I'm well aware that, at present, Your Excellency is principally concerned with the international situation, as is only right and proper. Your Excellency is accustomed to a wider perspective, to taking a much broader view of the world than us poor provincial politicians. But my friends in Palermo, who are also loyal friends of Your Excellency, entreat you through me to lower your gaze onto the Bank of Sicily, which, if Your Excellency does not intervene, seems destined to become the Palermo branch of a massive central bank, based in Rome and controlled by Northerners . . ."

When he heard the words "Bank of Sicily", His Excellency's

smile faded. His face became as still as a statue's and he stared into the other man's eyes as if to read his mind.

"What is going to happen to the Bank, Your Excellency?" asked The Swan. "We're afraid that something which belongs to us, and to the whole of Sicily, is going to be taken away. Our friends on the Bank's board are the ones who worry the most, Your Excellency. They spent so many years of their lives and so much energy fighting unsuccessfully against that old goat Notarbartolo, only to see the fruit of all their efforts slip from their grasp precisely when they were hoping to enjoy it . . ." He lowered his voice and went on: "Of course Your Excellency is not obliged to deal with such trifles, but the political struggle in Palermo really has become very bitter . . . If Giolitti and his Piedmontese ministers succeed in their evil scheme to abolish the Bank of Sicily's autonomy, Notarbartolo's death will have been pointless, and we'll have run so many risks for nothing . . ."

The Swan's voice had now sunk to a whisper and he was looking at His Excellency as if expecting some sign of agreement, but Francesco Crispi had stopped listening. The Bank's fate was already sealed in any case. He was lost in his own thoughts – that little man in front of him, dressed and coiffed like a provincial artist, had reminded him of an incident two years previously when, on the wall of a palace close to Palazzo Braschi in Rome, there had appeared the words: "Long live Francesco Crispi, head of the Mafia."

"There you are," His Excellency was thinking. "If there was a foreign journalist in the room with us, sufficiently well versed in Italian affairs to understand what this wretch is trying to say to me, he'd assume I really was the head of the Mafia. And in a sense he'd be right – but only in a sense, because whenever I've used the so-called Mafia (or anything else for that matter) it has always been for one purpose alone: the unity and glory of Italy. Also there are many others in Italy who aspire to control the Mafia these days – it's not just me any more. Even Rudiní and Giolitti (though he's Piedmontese) are getting involved in Mafia business. But they are mere sorcerer's apprentices, who will be destroyed by the demon they have summoned. Only a large-scale political plan, sustained by an immense determination to succeed, can overcome hundreds of thousands of personal and local interests, and the infinite network of collusion, silence, solidarity and group loyalty which binds those interests together."

When The Swan finished speaking and sat expectantly twisting the ends of his moustache, His Excellency straightened himself in his chair and looked at his visitor as if seeing him for the first time.

"Don't let's confuse things!" he warned. "In a constitutional state such as ours, one's political judgment of a man, and that same man's death, are two distinct, irreconcilable issues which most emphatically cannot be connected. Politically, Notarbartolo was a dwarf: one of those people I call Micro-maniacs, because only narrow horizons and restricted views ever enthuse them. The economic ambition of the present head of the Micromanic Party, Giovanni Giolitti, goes no further than the balance of payments. In foreign policy he believes in risking nothing and gaining nothing . . . As if those who simply do no harm and fail to act in their own best interests will be respected for it and given what is rightfully theirs! That is plainly not the case in the community of nations any more than among individuals."

For a moment His Excellency's gaze had wandered to a point in the wallpaper just above his guest's head, but now he met The Swan's eyes again and enunciated slowly and clearly:

"I never liked Notarbartolo while he was alive, but his end horrified me. Poor man! If I'd been Interior Minister when the crime was committed on the train, my instructions to the

Palermo Prefect, the Chief of Police and the whole of his force would have landed the real culprits in gaol, not simply one of their accomplices." He reflected a moment, then went on: "When the news of the murder reached Rome, last February, the first thing they said in parliamentary circles and newspaper offices was that Notarbartolo had been killed by my Sicilian friends, on my instructions . . . Political malice knows no bounds! The fact is that the man had left the public arena two years before and had no chance of coming back, at least not as director of the Bank of Sicily. What possible reason could I have had to hate him so much? As for the banks – the reform of our financial institutions is a missing element in the unity of our nation. I myself would have liked to resolve the matter when I was Head of Government, but they didn't give me the time."

The Swan was bemused. His Excellency, after years of milking the banks for all they were worth, was now claiming to head the moralising faction and to be eager to clean up the system . . . He opened his mouth to speak, then thought better of it and sat in silence. Francesco Crispi, on the other hand, was smiling again. He stood up, went over to the window and looked out, shielding his eyes with his hand to protect them from the glare of the sun off the sea, that stretched out incandescent beyond the dunes. He motioned Palizzolo over to join him.

"There are many ways to make money," His Excellency said, pointing at something in the avenue below the hotel windows – an advertising hoarding whose slogan The Swan could not decipher without his spectacles. "I'm going to show you one of them. See that hoarding? Signor Bertelli, from Milan, head of the firm which bears his name, realized some years ago that in the cities of Southern Italy people are terrified of cholera, particularly during the summer. So he invented an anti-cholera soap – Crelium, a disinfectant containing creolin. That poster – you may not be able to read it from here, but I can see it perfectly – says that Crelium can prevent cholera. There's also a picture of a woman holding a bar of their product – a perfectly normal soap, which differs from others only insofar as it costs twice as much and smells unpleasant.

"Two years ago, when I was Prime Minister, I made some inquiries at the Ministry of Industry and Commerce and discovered that this Signor Bertelli, inventor of the anti-cholera soap, is making millions in all the Southern cities – Naples, Messina, Palermo, Catania – just by investing a small sum in an advertising and commercial venture which, in itself, has nothing illegal about it. After all, nobody can deny that personal hygiene helps prevent all sorts of illnesses, including cholera, and this stinking soap isn't being sold in pharmacies as a medicine, but in grocery shops, like any normal soap. It's just a money-making exercise, but it works . . ."

He moved away from the window, but The Swan stayed there and felt a vast anger well up inside himself at the man who had made use of him for more than ten years, in Rome and particularly Palermo, to finance his politics and all sorts of other deals, but now clearly didn't need him any more, to judge by this gibberish.

"Who gives a toss," The Swan thought irritably, "about Crelium soap, cholera, and that bloody Milanese who makes millions advertising on the street!" He felt tempted to ask His Excellency why he hadn't gone to Bertelli for the money to pay the Bank of Rome's bills, but his courage failed him – nobody in the whole of Italy, not even the King, dared interrupt His Excellency while he was talking.

"I know for a fact," said His Excellency, "that throughout this great united Italy of ours there are millions of men like Bertelli: resourceful, enterprising and opportunistic; capable of creating wealth for themselves and for their country. I also know that a lot of them are Southerners who cannot display their qualities because the money has always been kept locked away in banks by Micromaniacs like Sella and Giolitti ... Italians are the most resourceful, enterprising people in the world, and if they'd had the support of the banks, our young nation would today have the same drive and vitality as the United States of America. Because this path – the path of enterprise and courage – is a nation's principal route to progress, wealth and economic and military power!"

The Swan made a wry face, thinking: "Here we go. He's on to world politics." It was common knowledge that His Excellency always finished his speeches by discussing Italy's role in the world, and this time was no exception.

"Our banking system must be changed," he boomed at the wallpaper just behind The Swan's head. "If I am made Prime Minister again, I will see to it personally. A nation like Italy cannot wait much longer for reform without risking the paralysis and collapse of its productive energies. I will bring a blast of fresh air to the economy! I have nothing but contempt for weaklings like Giolitti who believe that the Italy of Garibaldi and Mazzini should live like a petty-bourgeois, a humble clerk who begrudges every penny spent on housekeeping and dares not do or say anything that might upset his superiors. If she but wills it, Italy can become a leader in every sphere of human endeavour! As it is, our faint-hearts here at home turn pale and tear their hair out every time we receive a threat from whichever foreign power happens to be militarily stronger than us."

International politics – The Swan thought to himself – was to His Excellency what the music of Giuseppe Verdi's *Othello* was to the tenor Tamagno; but two discreet taps on the sitting-room door and the appearance of Palumbo Cardella's bald head stopped His Excellency in full flow. Crispi shifted his gaze from the wallpaper to his secretary's face, and made a gesture that meant "I'll be with you straight away", then bade

The Swan farewell without shaking his hand or even looking at him:

"Dear Palizzolo, I'm afraid I really have to leave you. Do come again . . ."

4

Marineo, 3 January 1894

Filicetta was running from street to street, clutching to her breast the shawl she was wearing against the cold and damp of the winter's day. As she ran she listened to voices coming from the Town Hall – the uproar from the crowd that had gathered in the square to shout:

"Long live Socialism! Down with the Mayor! Death to the toffs!" and other slogans which merged into one indistinct, unbroken yell down there among the houses. When she arrived in front of the great white bulk of La Matrice she stopped, uncertain what to do next. On the steps up to the church and under the portico she saw a large group of women who, like her, had been forbidden by their husbands to leave the house, but had come here nonetheless, to pray and to be close to their men in case of need. They were all in black from head to toe, wrapped up in shawls and whispering, even though there was nobody to overhear them . . .

"Jesus and Mary, *Za* Filicetta! Come and join us. We've got to stick together!"

The girl crossed the square to the group of women, and recognised *Za* Peppa, *Za* Nina, *Cummari* Rusidda, *Cummari* Gesualda and *Za* Biniditta (*Za* and *Cummari* are roughly equivalent to Aunty and Grandma, but used for all women irrespective of family ties). Each of them was either wife or mother to one of those impoverished peasants who – like her own husband Saro – had founded a Worker's *Fascio* in Marineo one spring day of the previous year and who now were down there in front of the Town Hall, calling for the abolition of tax on flour and the right to live in a slightly less unjust world . . . Small workers' action groups with Socialist and Anarchist leanings, named *Fasci*, had been springing up all over Sicily in the past year. What high hopes, Filicetta reflected, had been born with them in Marineo and the whole of Sicily! And how many arguments had raged around the oil-lamps in the evening, because the women did not want their men to go to meetings rumoured to attract "Women Communists" from Palermo, or even the north of Italy, who preached free love: one aspect of Socialism which, the women yelled, would not catch on in Sicily, not in a million years, and if the man in their house took it into his head to sleep with a Communist, even just once, blood would be spilt. Before every meeting the men had to muster all their eloquence and swear on the heads of their children and dead relatives that the stories of Women Communists were fairy tales circulated by the toffs and the priests to discredit them. But to be on the safe side, some of the women would accompany their men to the headquarters of the *Fascio* and remain on guard there, saying their rosary, until it was time to go home.

At those meetings there was much talk of a future in which all men and women, whatever their position at birth, would become masters of their lives and their labour. Listening to her husband Saro's words, Filicetta too had come to believe that the world would soon change for the better. When Carmelo Giordano the cobbler (nicknamed *Zitamentu* because he was also the town marriage broker) came round to their house in the evenings and spoke of a certain Karl Marx, the revolution of the proletariat, and a future in which all inequalities and abuses of power would be abolished, she listened to him in wide-eyed, gaping wonder, just as she had when her grandfather told her stories as a child. She would leave the room only if Nuzzu, her new-born son, started crying, or if Saro waved her away because he and his friends were going to discuss "men's business". Recent meetings, in particular, had generated an atmosphere of conspiracy and imminent danger which alarmed the women and made them anxious for their men's safety. The toffs from the Club and the Town Hall did not want the world to change. Supporting the toffs and the status quo were the priests (*parrini*), who dealt in the here and now as well as the hereafter and, almost without exception, sided with the rich; the tenant farmers (*gabellotti*) who carved up the landed estates of the aristocracy between them; the *curatoli* and *liuni* who went around with guns slung over their shoulders, and treated the peasants worse than animals; the King's *carabinieri* – the Pigs – who behaved threateningly towards the Socialists, and toadied to the swells and the priests; and finally the army, which had arrived in the last few days. Troops had shot into crowds in different parts of the island, and in Marineo the previous day they had used bayonets to welcome protesters from Belmonte Mezzagno who had come to support the locals. But fear hadn't arrived at Marineo with the army – it had already been present for several months. After the strikes and the sabotage of the previous year's harvest, there had appeared in the town, as in nearby Piana dei Greci, Giardinello and Belmonte Mezzagno, a couple of characters of the type whose mere appearance puts the fear of God into you – one Don Piddu, nicknamed *Facci di lignu*, and one Don Calo nicknamed *Chiaccu* (Hangman's knot) because his speciality, according to those in the know, was to hang his victims so that their death looked like suicide . . . They would turn up when least expected with their gangs of thugs on horseback, all armed to the teeth, take up position in front of the *Fascio* headquarters or *Zitamentu*'s shop and beat up anyone going in or out, assault women and generally intimidate people without the *carabinieri* ever considering it necessary to intervene. The *carabinieri* and the Mafia's *liuni* – the peasants said – had declared an armistice, if not actually a partnership, ever since the founding of the first *Fascio*, and it would take a lot more than a Socialist being beaten up or even killed to get them to shoot at each other.

Cummari Rusidda was drying her tears.

"Holy Mary, mother of God," she prayed, "make sure nothing happens to our men! Santa Rosalia, help them!"

Suddenly the shouts and clamour of the crowd down there beyond the network of streets and alleyways died down to nothing. A long silence fell, which terrified the women. Many knelt down, hands joined in prayer, facing the church doors which the parish priest had taken the precaution to shut and bolt. All of them, including Filicetta, crossed themselves. One or two even raised their hands to cover their ears, but nothing happened. All they heard was a man's voice. "It's the Mayor," some of them said. "That scoundrel! It's the Mayor speaking." Then came an explosion of joy from the crowd, followed by a long round of applause and a cry of triumph:

"Victory! Victory! Long live Socialism!"

Bewildered and incredulous, the women shook their heads and looked at each other. Could it really all be over, their eyes asked; had the toffs and the town council yielded on the matter of tax, just when the army had arrived to support them? After a moment's silence they heard another voice, which they recognised at once. "It's the president of the *Fascio*!" they exclaimed. "It's *Zu* Tonino!" When this new voice stopped there was an even longer burst of applause: a veritable ovation.

"Long live the *Fasci*! Up with Socialism!"

"Long live *Zu* Tonino Marretta!"

Different voices were now yelling from the alleyways:

"A procession! The whole town in procession to celebrate the workers' victory! *Zu* Tonino Marretta will make a speech!"

The women began to run towards the Town Hall, and the square in front of the church was left deserted. Filicetta set off for the *Fascio* headquarters, hoping to find Saro there, although she knew in her heart that she wouldn't. She saw *Zitamentu* being carried in triumph by a hundred or so peasants and day labourers, who were shouting:

"Long live Socialism!"

She saw the town band lined up in the middle of a street, running through the "Hymn to Garibaldi" and other patriotic tunes, without sparing their lungs nor the brass section. When she got to the *Fascio* office she looked into its single ground-floor room, but Saro wasn't there. She carried on and, at the corner of the square, met a small band of *liuni* with guns slung over their shoulders. In their midst was a man Filicetta immediately recognised, because he had been terrorising the peasants of Marineo for months, and because he had the kind of face not easily forgotten after even a single meeting: Don Piddu *Facci di lignu*. She turned off the street in a panic and found herself in the square, among the crowd which was already starting to disperse. Some people were looking for friends to help celebrate the tax victory; some were heading for the Town Hall where the thanksgiving procession was to start; others were just going home. Beneath the Mayor's windows two or three hundred people were still occasionally shouting "Up with the Fasci", "Down with the toffs" and "Long live Socialism", but without much conviction: simply to help pass the time as they waited for the band to arrive.

The Mayor and a few other local gentry were out on the balcony. They were smoking fat cigars, Filicetta noticed, and laughing with satisfaction as if they, and not the peasants, had won the day. All round the Town Hall, protecting the nobs barricaded inside and defending the building from a possible attack by the rabble, stood the *carabinieri* and the soldiers, ready for battle. The *carabinieri*, who were less numerous, were guarding the entrance with muskets and revolvers, while the soldiers, lined up three deep, were wielding rifles so enormously tall that they looked like halberds, with fixed bayonets. They were wearing greatcoats, too long and too heavy for the mild Sicilian winter, and their expressions were those of frightened, or perhaps sulking, children. On the other side of the avenue stood the Socialists with their *Fascio* banner. Saro was among them, and Filicetta raised her hand to attract his attention, but didn't manage it because at precisely that moment someone shoved her in the back so hard that she almost fell. She turned and recognised one of Don Piddu's men, a tall thin fellow with a scar on his face, who elbowed his way through the rest of the crowd until he reached the line of *carabinieri*, which he spat at.

Filicetta was petrified but had time to notice two things: firstly, when she'd seen that man in the alley he'd been holding a gun, while now he was unarmed, and secondly, the toffs had disappeared from the Town Hall balcony and the window was shut. Then the stranger shouted at the *carabinieri*:

"May you all die before nightfall! Stinking vermin!"

A great hush fell in front of the Town Hall. The band could be heard in the distance playing a hymn, "Salve regina fulgida", one of the mainstays of their repertoire. Somebody said: "He's a troublemaker," and the word circulated throughout the crowd. Many tongues repeated it, but nobody had the courage or presence of mind to act – and in any case, what could they possibly have done? Everybody stood on tiptoe to get a look at the stranger's face, but saw only the heads and caps of the people in front. Those in the first few rows, though they vaguely sensed they were in danger, stood gaping at the *carabinieri* and at the man who was cursing, as if they were watching puppets in one of the travelling shows which occasionally stopped off even in Marineo and, right there in front of the Town Hall, told wondrous tales of challenges and duels that lasted three days and three nights . . .

The eyes which the captain of the *carabinieri* fixed on the stranger had become two very thin slits in his round and apparently impassive face. The foreigner spat at him a second time, then turned to the young conscripts, bundled up in their ridiculous winter uniforms. He pulled a copper coin from his pocket and threw it at their feet, sneering, while their commanding officer pulled at his blond moustache with his left hand and fingered his holster with the right.

"What are you doing here in Sicily?" the stranger shouted. "Go to Africa to straighten out the Negroes' bananas, like your mates have! Go to Dogali!"

He turned to the crowd. Not a sound could be heard in the square or the avenue and nobody, not even those at the very back, had any trouble hearing the man with the disfigured face who had never been seen in Marineo before that day.

"You're all sheep!" the scarred man shouted. "Act like men, if you've got the balls! Show these swine you won't let anyone push you around in your home town, in front of your women!" He pointed towards the corner of the square where the other *liuni* stood and shouted at them: "Anyone with a gun, use it. I'm going to get mine!"

His performance over, the foreigner calmly turned round and, ignoring the infantry officer who had drawn his pistol, elbowed his way back into the middle of the bewildered crowd and disappeared as suddenly as he'd arrived. Then, from the street corner where Filicetta remembered having seen Don Piddu, a shot rang out; then another, then another. Everybody felt as if time had slowed to a halt; as if the air had turned to glass. Filicetta wanted to open her mouth and shout "Saro! Saro!", but she couldn't. Everything stood still, petrified by the horror of that terrible moment. Even the band had stopped playing. Only after the echo of the last shot had died out among the houses did people and events begin to move again: the crowd scattered, yelling, as the captain of the *carabinieri* lifted a large revolver in both hands and aimed at those closest to him, and the army officer barked out those three terrible words which Filicetta did not hear that first time, but which to the ears of the frightened young soldiers must have sounded like so many cracks of a whip:

"Load! Aim! Fire!"

A few isolated shots rang out, while people crowded together and clambered over each other, no longer seeing or understanding anything – they yelled in terror as they tried to escape. Then came the first volley of gunfire and the whole square was filled with a cloud of acrid yellow smoke. Filicetta found herself pressed between a wall and a closed door, without knowing how she'd got there. When the smoke ahead of her cleared, she saw a large number of bodies on the ground – dozens of men and a few women. Some were screaming, kicking, bouncing on the cobbles as if they had an invisible spring inside them; some were dying, their mouths yawning open, or tearing their nails and fingertips on the paving stones as they tried desperately to grasp on to the thing that was slipping away from them, though they no longer even knew what that thing was; still others were lying motionless in grotesque positions, arms and legs askew, their staring eyes asking one last question: "What has happened to me?"

The *Fascio* banner had fallen to the ground, and next to it lay Saro, a dark stain in the middle of his shirt and his mouth gaping wide – stone dead, though his legs, from the knee down, were still moving like the limbs of a puppet knight in the travelling shows. Many people were running among the bodies, treading on them and tripping over them; many of those on the ground were trying desperately to escape, doing their utmost to squirm along by pushing themselves forward with those parts of their bodies which still worked . . .

"Load! Aim! Fire!"

This time Filicetta heard the officer's words as she was running towards Saro, then felt herself being touched on the shoulder – a discreet tap, as if someone were trying to warn her of a danger. She looked round and found herself lying on the ground next to a distant relative, a day labourer whom everybody in the town called *Piriteddu* (little fart) because of his size and the smell he had acquired through working with manure.

"Why am I lying on the ground with this man?" she wondered. She tried to get up, but her arms and legs refused to respond. She passed out and lay motionless where she'd fallen, her clothes in an unseemly mess and one arm round *Piriteddu*'s waist.

There was a painful sound in her ears. She opened her eyes and realized it was a woman keening, a few feet from where she lay. Her wailing was so excruciatingly high-pitched that, if the man hadn't been dead, Filicetta thought to herself, he'd have got up and run away. She saw another woman on her knees beside a corpse, rocking backwards and forwards, revelling in the pain of an endless dirge in which she repeated the dead man's name hundreds of times: "Janu, Janu . . ."

Filicetta lifted her arm off *Piriteddu* and, feeling how cold and stiff his body was, realized he was dead. She propped herself up on her elbow and noticed she had lost a lot of blood: beneath her left shoulder her clothes and shawl were soaked through and there was a large stain on the cobbles. She wondered why, if she was wounded, she didn't feel any pain, but couldn't find an answer. She looked around. The sky was still overcast yet bright as it had been when she left home, and the town seemed to be deserted: the *carabinieri* and soldiers were gone and every door was bolted, every window shut . . . The only presence on the streets were those women, black as birds of ill-omen, standing or kneeling next to their dead and shouting their desperation at them. There was also a priest, equally black from head to toe, who was tracing the sign of the cross and muttering a prayer over each body.

Looking at the priest and listening to the keeners, Filicetta remembered that Saro was dead. She tried to stand up, but couldn't, so she gritted her teeth and began to drag herself, face downwards, towards the place where she had last seen her husband. She passed a woman who was tearing at her clothes and scratching her face as she shouted:

"Oh Gnaziu! Gnaziu! How are we going to manage without you? Oh Gnaziu! Gnaziu! How are we going to live? Oh Gnaziu! Gnaziu! Gnaziu! . . ."

Another, kneeling next to the corpse of a boy, was softly singing his praises:

"You were as pretty as a ray of sunlight," she told him, "you were as good as a fine day, you were as good as freshly-baked bread, you were as good as the Easter joint of lamb . . ."

The red banner of the *Fascio* was no longer lying among the victims; someone must have come to take it away. Saro, however, was still there, as pale as if he'd turned to chalk. A fly was walking over his chin and lips, buzzing from one cheek to the other, flying away and returning with the annoying persistence of its kind. Filicetta pulled herself up next to her husband and sat looking at him or, to be more precise, sat looking at the fly. Her head suddenly felt empty and vast – a cavern or a deserted valley echoing with the wails of the keening women, who were weeping on her behalf too. She should have closed the dead man's eyes; she should have waved that wretched fly away, but the emptiness in her head continued to grow and she slowly lost consciousness and slumped over Saro's body.

She lifted her head again and it was dark. The street-lamps had not been lit in the hushed, deserted town, but the clouds above the houses had thinned out and the moon floated in its own light as if in transparent fluid, infinitely remote from the affairs of men. The keeners and the priest had gone; many of the bodies had also disappeared. The sounds she heard now were the sounds of the night. An owl hooted before crossing the small patch of sky between two houses; somewhere towards the square a wounded man groaned; then she heard growling and snarling, like a pack of dogs fighting over food. She looked in the direction of the noise and realized with horror that the object the dogs were tearing at and trying to drag away was the arm of a child or a very small man, and that a body was attached to it . . . *Piriteddu*! She tried to sit up, but couldn't. The wound on her shoulder was hurting and her head, empty and light before, was now immensely heavy – so heavy that her neck and shoulders could barely support it. She felt cold – horribly cold – and she realized that her thoughts had become rapid and disjointed, as in a dream.

"Could I be dreaming?" she asked herself. "Could all this be a nightmare?"

She heard a low whistle, the sound of many footsteps and the baying of dogs running off towards the square. From a vast distance she sensed someone leaning over her and touching her very gently – turning her over, taking her pulse . . . A voice said:

"It's *Za* Filicetta! She's still alive," and another whispered in her ear: "It's all right, Filicetta . . . we're friends. We're taking you home."

5

Towards Palermo, 8 May 1894

Through the carriage window and the dust raised by the coaches ahead of hers, Giuseppina Crispi gazed out at Sicily, a place about which, from earliest childhood, she had heard nothing but marvels. Everybody born there – including her mother and her father Francesco – talked of Sicily as a wondrous, fantastical land, where extremes meet and coexist, where all the beauties of creation reveal themselves to the incredulous eyes of the traveller . . . Instead of which, the landscape she had been looking at for quite a number of days was the bleakest and most monotonous imaginable, at least in Italy. A landscape smothered in dust, dry and bare even before the onset of summer: and this was in spring, the most beautiful season of the year. All around her were grey or yellow hills of volcanic rock without a single tree and, clinging to their slopes or perched on the hilltops, absurd, hazy villages which nobody in their right mind – the girl thought – would ever choose to live in. You'd have to have suffered the misfortune to be born there . . .

Was this the magical Sicily people talked about? Three years earlier, in 1891, when she had accompanied her father to Palermo to visit the National Exhibition, the place had struck her very differently. Carriage drives along the Marina, evenings at the theatre, dances and society life in general had not disappointed her – on the contrary it had seemed to her that the fashionable world in Sicily compared favourably with that of

Naples or Rome. But Palermo was Palermo – a large city, whose aristocracy was related to all the other European aristocracies; the people she met on that visit she saw again in Rome and Naples and would have seen in Paris too, had she gone there . . . The island of Sicily, on the other hand, was this succession of volcanic hills, this barren, sulphurous land where the grass seemed to come up already dead and even the houses of the aristocracy – when you finally reached them after hours and hours on rough, potholed roads – felt pointlessly grand and depressing. And the inhabitants were worthy of the place. The men and women who lived in those ghostly dwellings, with their endless empty rooms and mildewed, termite-ridden salons, were almost all hideous – monsters who were striving, each in their own way and for their own secret reasons, to disprove Darwin's theory and demonstrate that man is not descended from the apes, but vice versa . . . As they travelled from one large mansion to the next on those dusty sheep-tracks which Sicilians called roads, they constantly encountered soldiers – artillerymen, infantrymen and riflemen who marched along raising vast clouds of dust and whose grimy, exhausted appearance brought tears to the eyes of Giuseppina's lady companions ("So young and so far from home! Poor boys!"). The girl had no idea what all those soldiers could possibly be protecting in that desert of dust, stones and godforsaken villages. To tell the truth she couldn't begin to imagine. All she knew, having heard it repeated at least a hundred times since she landed, was that martial law and a curfew had been imposed on the island, and the soldiers one saw all over the place had been sent by the Government (that is to say her father, Francesco Crispi) to suppress the Socialist insurrection led by the "Workers' *Fasci*".

From time to time in that bleak landscape Giuseppina would see shepherds dressed from head to toe in sheepskins, and peasants – barefoot, almost naked and half the size of normal men – who repelled her. Could these really be the famous men of Sicily, those fiery lovers, those irresistible seducers of women she'd heard so much about from her female acquaintances in the drawing rooms of Rome? In the whole of this pilgrimage across Sicily she had seen only one really handsome man: a bronze Adonis who looked as if he'd stepped out of a history book . . . She closed her eyes to visualise him. He had appeared before her suddenly, sitting on a painted cart. His hair was black and curly, his eyes dark and, as he passed close to Giuseppina, he looked at her so insolently that she felt herself being stripped naked by his gaze – a not altogether unpleasant sensation. Then, as the cart disappeared in a cloud of dust, her Adonis began to sing in Sicilian dialect at the top of his voice:

"I saw a woman like a flag; she hid the sun and moon"

The song had continued in the distance, but those were the only words she could make out. Remembering that encounter Giuseppina reflected that, in an ideal world free of taboos, any woman would want to make love with that man, anywhere, without even asking his name – but there is no such thing as an ideal world, except in dreams. Real lives are complicated by an endless array of conventions and rules. In her case, she was about to get married – that is to promise to love just one man, who wasn't even a bronze Adonis, to the end of her days . . .

"What will happen once we've been married for a while?" she wondered. "In the long run, people hate each other . . ." She turned to the girl sitting next to her, who was withdrawn and silent, probably out of shyness. This girl, who wore her hair gathered in a bun at the nape of her neck, kept her eyes lowered and was dressed for the provinces, was her cousin Angela from Girgenti, who was accompanying her for part of the journey. The gentlewomen in Giuseppina's retinue – eagerly seizing the chance to gossip freely about their young mistress, her mother's infidelities and her father's pedigree as a cuckold – had put an entire coach at the disposal of the two cousins, so that they could travel alone.

"You must have so much to talk about at your age," they had said to the two girls, "so many secrets to confide!" But as yet neither of them had spoken a word. Giuseppina had no wish to reveal any secrets to a stranger she had met only once before, when they were children. Angela, on the other hand, would have given anything not to appear awkward in front of His Excellency's daughter, and was searching for some suitable opening with which to begin a conversation, some casual remark which had not yet come to her.

"And what about you, Angela?" Giuseppina asked, suddenly curious to know what middle-class Sicilian girls did before getting married. "Do you have a fiancé? Is he handsome?"

This question – in essence a continuation of her cousin's thoughts – took Angela by surprise and made her blush.

"Yes, I am engaged," she replied demurely. "We're getting married in a few years' time. At the moment he's studying law in Palermo, and he still has to get his degree. I don't know if he's handsome," she felt it her duty to add, as if repeating some virtuous line she'd learned from somebody (perhaps even her parents), "but I like him as he is and I wouldn't want him any other way."

"Will he be your first man?" her cousin asked. "I mean, when you get married, will you have made love to anyone else while he was away?"

This time Angela looked round abruptly, as if someone had stuck her with a hatpin. She found the courage to rebel:

"What do you mean? . . . Of course he'll be my first, and afterwards I'll be faithful to him for the rest of my life!" She stared at Giuseppina, wide-eyed. "Why are you asking me these things? What are you getting at?"

"What if he betrayed you?" her companion suggested. "You see, I'm about to get married, and it seems only right that a woman should ask herself certain questions. For instance, if you knew he was betraying you with a girl from Palermo or even a married woman, would you still feel you had to stay faithful to him?"

Angela raised her eyebrows. Her eyes flashed in the half-light of the carriage.

"If he betrayed me," she replied, without the slightest hesitation, "I'd stab them both – him, and the slut who tried to take him from me!"

Giuseppina stared at her in amazement, then lifted a hand as if to say "never mind, let's change the subject . . ." She thought of her father: how many men would the Prime Minister, Francesco Crispi, have to stab if he ever took it into his head to kill all his wife's past and present lovers?

She thought of the Principe di Linguaglossa and wondered whether her future husband believed he was about to marry a little virgin like Angela – or if anybody had taken the trouble to inform him that she, Giuseppina Crispi, had already had a number of affairs, one great passion, and, the previous year, had even allowed herself the luxury of a relationship with a man thirty-five years her senior, the deputy Pietro Antonelli, simply to find out what it felt like to steal a lover from her mother?

She looked out of the coach window, through the clouds of dust, at the hillside villages, and it occurred to her that up there people probably killed each other over the merest trifle: a furtive glance, a misunderstood word would provoke Heaven knows what massacres, in those ridiculous places. Such a primitive and barbarous attitude to love reminded her of an occasion a few days previously, when the Principe di Linguaglossa had taken her to visit a sulphur mine. Giuseppina had watched half-naked boys emerging one by one from a hole in the ground, bent double under the sacks of sulphur. Those poor unfortunates, staring at her with eyes that were too large and too black, unnerved her. Francesco had explained that they were *carusi*, helpers and slaves of the miners – the *pirriaturi* – to whom they had been sold before the age of ten. They went up and down the steps of the mine shaft all day long, loaded like donkeys, until darkness fell outside; then, at night, they were expected to share their master's bed, however repugnant that may sound. In the daytime they were servants and at night wives . . .

"You won't find a more depraved group of boys in the whole world," the Principe di Linguaglossa had told her, seizing one of them by his curly hair and shaking his head back and forth as he did with his dog Bakunin – an English setter he had named after the Russian anarchist. "Hardly a week goes by in these mining communities without some *pirriaturi* wounding or killing another because of a *caruso*. Then the *carusi* grow up and become *pirriaturi* themselves – generation after generation, the men who dig for sulphur are all the same . . ."

At the time Giuseppina had thought that a sulphur miner's life couldn't be all that dreadful if, at the end of a gruelling day, these men were still capable of passions strong enough to make them confront each other knife in hand. But before dawn the following morning, as she lay in a large four-poster bed in a Count's villa, she heard the distant sound of the miners singing on their way to work:

> "*Mamma nun mi mannati a la pirrera*
> *ca notti e jornu mi pigghiu tirrura . . .*"
> (Mother don't send me to the mines
> Day and night they terrify me . . .)

It was a sad song, sadder than any the girl had ever heard before. Giuseppina listened and, before she fell asleep again, remembered hearing her father tell very different stories about the sulphur mines – stories about men dying in their hundreds down in the pits, without the newspapers giving them a single inch of the space they lavished so generously on minor comedy actresses, opera singers and the most insignificant members of royal families. Even those who survived the firedamp and the roof-falls did not live beyond the age of fifty, because the sulphur destroyed their lungs.

The carriages slowed almost to a halt and Giuseppina stopped thinking about the miners. She opened her door and leant out to see what the trouble was, but all she saw was a cloud of dust and, inside that cloud, the captain of her escort spurring his horse towards her and waving her back inside.

"Ladies," the officer said, "I'm afraid I have to ask you to keep your doors shut and your curtains drawn and not to show yourselves. We're about to pass a group of prisoners who are being transferred on foot," he explained. "There's no danger, but we must follow regulations and put safety first."

The prisoners had somehow found out that Crispi's daughter was in one of the carriages and they were yelling at the tops of their voices:

"Have mercy on us! Tell the president we've done nothing wrong, pretty lady! We were asking for justice and they gave us bullets. Mercy! Mercy!"

"While we're in prison our children are dying of hunger!"

"Look out at us, Your Excellency – look what they've done to us! Tell your father about it!"

"They treat us worse than criminals! We're honest men!"

Disobeying the officer's instructions, the girl pulled back the curtain and looked out. She saw a long column of men chained in pairs, who were lifting their shackles for her to see and would have thrown themselves beneath the horses' hooves to stop the coaches, if there hadn't been soldiers there to restrain them. Those men, Giuseppina thought, must be the famous Socialists of the *Fasci* revolt which the army had been sent to suppress. They were so completely covered in white dust that they looked like the souls of the dead, stretching arms and faces out towards her, shouting their names and begging her to do something for them.

"I'm Nannu Gallina! I've got seven children!"

"I'm Carmine Cannizzo! My wife was killed by the King's soldiers. Tell His Excellency about me, pretty lady!"

"I'm Rosario Mancuso, from San Biagio Platani in the province of Girgenti! Tell His Excellency our worker's association was named after Francesco Crispi."

"We asked for bread and justice, and they slit our throats like pigs."

At the head of the column Giuseppina saw some prisoners who, even though they were as ragged and dusty as the rest, looked more like middle-class men and intellectuals than peasants. One in particular attracted her attention and struck her as amusing – a man of average height, with a forehead so high that it almost reached the top of his head, and little gold-rimmed glasses held together with a piece of string. Out of curiosity she turned to look at him and he, who had been one of the leaders of the revolt, assumed that she had recognised him. He began to wave his arms about and yell like one possessed.

"You must tell your father," the prisoner with the glasses shouted, trying to raise his voice above all the others, "that last summer these poor wretches in chains were cheering Crispi in every town square in Sicily. He can't abandon them now that he's Head of Government. Remember to tell him! It's important! Tell His Excellency we still believe in him, despite everything. Tell him to grant an amnesty, but for God's sake to grant it quickly!"

The horses broke into a trot again and the cries were left behind. Giuseppina returned her attention to the inside of the carriage and saw that Angela had removed a handkerchief from her sleeve and was using it to dry her tears.

"Why are you crying?" Giuseppina asked. "Did you recognise someone? Some relative of ours?"

The girl shook her head. She blew her nose to stifle a sob and murmured:

"Poor things! Their poor families!" Then she realized that her pity might be misconstrued and hurried to explain: "Of course they were wrong to besiege the town halls and burn down the toll-houses, but outsiders put them up to it. They're all honest people: peasants and factory workers, a few university students, some young graduates and clerks . . ."

There was a brief silence broken only by the tramp of horses' hooves and the sound of wheels on the unmade road.

"Will you talk to your father about it?" Angela asked. "Will you tell him what terrible conditions you saw them in, and ask him to help?"

Giuseppina burst out laughing and shook her head at her companion.

"What an idea!" she exclaimed. Then she became serious again. "Even if I did," she replied, "it'd be no use – my father would just change the subject. He's never discussed that sort of thing with me. And anyway not even someone like him can get people out of prison without good reason. It's complicated, even for a Prime Minister . . ."

She gazed out of the window. Was it still far to Palermo? She couldn't wait to reach the city and be done with these hills and all this dust, these scenes of misery and oppression . . . She was going to have to have a serious talk with Francesco before she married him. All her life she had lived between two capitals, Rome and Naples. She would never be able to adapt to living like the Sicilian aristocrats she had met over the past few days – the Count and Countess of Sulphur Volcanoes, the Duke and Duchess of Dust and Salt-Mines, the Prince and Princess of Dry Grass, the Marquis of Malaria and his late-lamented consort, carried off by that disease . . .

A few weeks in Palermo or on the Taormina coast every year before summer started was the most she would be able to stand. In the other seasons she wanted to settle in Rome or Naples, be seen at the theatre, attend balls, visit her friends and society people . . . Nobody, not even a husband, would compel her to bury herself in such a backwater as Sicily, where there was nothing, or next to nothing, to amuse her.

It was past midday. The sun was now directly above them, beating straight down on to the black shells of the carriages and making them unbearably hot. The landscape through the window, however, was marginally less dry and barren than it had appeared in the early hours of the morning. Along the side of the road there were a few eucalyptus trees; to their right there was a hill that was almost green, with horses grazing on it and, in the distance, a pale blue and violet hamlet, whose tiny houses clustered round a fortified convent. There was a stream with a little water in each of its puddles and a shady valley below a cliff. The carriages stopped. The men jumped out first, dusting off their clothes and joking amongst themselves and with the ladies, who were pretending to be unable to get down without their help. The Principe di Linguaglossa ran to open the door of Giuseppina and Angela's carriage, helped them out, and would certainly have stayed to talk had he not been hailed by a distant relative, the elderly Marchesa di Avola, who was insisting on being helped by him alone. The girls looked around to see where they had got to and all of a sudden Angela's face lit up and she clapped her hands with almost childlike joy. She seized her cousin by the arm:

"Look down there! The *ciuri de maju* are in flower! How lovely!"

Giuseppina turned round in surprise and saw the "March flowers" – a golden cloud on the other side of a little bridge over the stream. Angela took her hand and she – young city lady that she was, accustomed to having every kind of flower delivered to her house – found herself standing among those mysterious stems, as tall as they themselves were, or even taller. "What's come over her?" she asked herself. "And why have I followed her into this field?" But she could find no answer.

There were as many as ten or twelve *ciuri de maju* on each stem, and in no time at all Angela had picked a large bunch which she gave to Giuseppina.

"They're good luck for everyone," she explained, "but particularly for you, because you're getting married. They're a symbol of abundance. Where I come from we say that every one of these flowers is a gold coin and that any wish you make while you're standing among them will come true." She picked another bunch for herself, then turned back to her cousin.

"What are you waiting for?" she asked impatiently. "Make a wish – ask for anything you want and it'll be granted, just you wait and see . . ."

Purgatory (1896–1899)

I

Palermo, 25 October 1896

Filicetta was crying. For half an hour, perhaps even an hour, she had been curled up in a corner of the sofa, hiding her face in the crook of her arm. The tears brought a sense of relief which she couldn't have explained. She wasn't crying about anything in particular. She no longer even remembered the fright she'd had a little while before, when she opened her front door and found herself face to face with somebody she would have preferred never to set eyes on again, there or anywhere else. Also vanished were the memories which the mere sight of that man had evoked, even though for a short time they had assailed her with all the force of a physical sensation. She was crying for the childhood and adolescence of a country girl who had accidentally got caught up in the *Fasci* riots, then had ceased to exist, because she turned into a different person. She was crying for the past of the Filicetta she no longer was: her dead husband, her sons Saro and Nuzzu who now lived with their grandparents, her relatives, her girlfriends, the people she used to know. She was crying for the town below the cliff and for the mountains which, for twenty years, had been home to the girl who bore her name . . .

Filicetta was a city lady now, in her small third-floor flat in Via dei Biscottari, with its cage of budgies on the balcony and pot of basil by the front door. But the transformation had taken some time. She had arrived in Palermo one January morning in 1894, a year which now felt immensely distant, her teeth chattering with the cold and the fever induced by the wound in her shoulder. She had been forced to hide in the home of an elderly couple, two "comrades" who had gladly volunteered to take her in because her name appeared on the list of insurgents who, on General Morra's instructions, were being hunted all over the island and tried in military courts. Those good people had treated her like a daughter. Only after many months, when she was fully recovered and things were returning to normal in Palermo, did they advise her to go to the Honourable Raffaele Palizzolo, Member of Parliament for the city's Albergaria district, for assistance with her legal problems.

"Palizzolo is a politician who's very close to Francesco Crispi, the Prime Minister," her benefactors told her. "He's also a great mafioso and friend of mafiosi. But if you can touch his heart, he's the only man in Palermo who can get you out of this mess."

The Honourable Member received his petitioners in the offices of his "Election Committee", on the ground floor of a building in Piazza del Carmine. Filicetta went there and queued up with everyone else. When her turn came to be heard by the great man, she told him all her misfortunes, from Saro's death to her present wretchedness. She couldn't carry on like this, she said through her tears: living in hiding and being supported by two old people who could barely support themselves, and who were risking imprisonment because of her. It was a very hot day in late June; Palizzolo listened to Filicetta without interrupting, frowning occasionally and staring at a point in her blouse at the level of her bosom, from which she kept removing and replacing the handkerchief she was using to dry her tears.

It wasn't the girl's fault of course, but it just so happened that – as well as sweet, regular features and eyes as black as her hair – Mother Nature had endowed her with two large breasts, which the Honourable Member was contemplating in an entranced daze. When she came to the end of her story and sat looking at him tearfully, The Swan signalled his assent two or three times with a nod which involved not just his head but the whole of his body. He immediately assured her of his deep concern, twirling the ends of his moustache between his fingertips and wholeheartedly taking her side.

"It cannot be right," he declared forcefully, raising his forefinger, "for such a young and beautiful lady to suffer because of a misunderstanding and a crime she has not committed!" He took down Filicetta's name and the address of her hosts, so that he could contact her as soon as he had any news. He rose to show her to the door, and it was only then that Filicetta realized how small the great man actually was: at least four or five inches shorter than herself. At the door he bowed, took the girl's hand, and pressed it lingeringly to his lips, looking into her eyes as if to say: "You needn't worry. Your troubles are over; I'm here to take care of you."

The following morning, only a few hours after that first meeting, Filicetta received a visit from a certain Signora Ancila, doyenne of Albergaria madams, who introduced herself with the words: "You lucky little minx! You've fallen on your feet, my girl, and more fool you if you don't take advantage of it!"

She then explained that "His Excellency" the Honourable Member ("A man of gold, Filicetta, take it from someone who's known him since he was in short trousers! A man who only has to say a word, in Palermo or Rome, to get whatever he wants!") was going to raise her case with General Morra as soon as possible. In the meantime, however, Filicetta's eyes had bewitched him and it would be wrong for her to let him suffer agonies of love when she had the power to bring happiness to both of them. The Honourable Member was like that, Signora Ancila said: at the age of forty-five he still fell in love like a teenager, and he would be waiting for her at precisely nine o'clock that evening at the "Election Committee's" offices in

Piazza del Carmine. He wasn't promising her jewellery or money, because he knew he was dealing with a respectable woman and didn't want to risk offending her, but she, Ancila, could assure Filicetta that she wouldn't regret keeping the appointment. Well? What was she waiting for to show her delight and thank Heaven for such a stroke of luck? Filicetta had been staring vacantly at Signora Ancila as she spoke, so the Madam gave her a warning:

"Watch yourself, young woman! Don't be stupid about this. Remember: '*Na vota scinni fortuna di lu celu!*'" (Heaven rains down good luck but once).

The girl spent the afternoon sitting in the shady part of the courtyard in a run-down block of flats, watching children play hide-and-seek, asking herself: "Should I go? What should I do?" But she already knew she would keep the appointment. She was tired of having to rely on people who shared their pittance with her for the sake of Socialism, an ideal she no longer believed in. She was tired of hiding; tired of living in fear of being sent to court and given ten or twenty years . . . What did a woman like her have left to lose in any case? Her honest life, her dreams, her dignity had all died up there in front of the Town Hall, in the place she could not return to for fear of arrest – the place where, most importantly, she had no wish to return.

For the first time since her husband's death, Filicetta was realizing that something inside her had changed for ever; that she would never go back to Marineo, not even for the sake of her children. Furthermore (and this may have been what most surprised her about the strange, reprehensible thoughts she was having) the prospect of becoming the mistress of a rich and influential man did not fill her with her all the revulsion it should have. To tell the truth it looked like the only way out of a predicament which might otherwise become really desperate . . . A stroke of luck, just as Signora Ancila had said.

As for Palizzolo, he seemed harmless enough – really quite a funny little man, with his diminutive round face, his paunch and his falsetto. Perhaps going to bed with such a homunculus, the girl thought to herself, was more an act of charity than a proper sin . . .

When the sun began to set, Filicetta dressed as smartly as she could and walked down from Porta Carini to Piazza del Carmine, keeping to the back alleys so as to avoid soldiers who might stop her and ask her name. The Honourable Member received her in his dressing gown and showed her into a sitting room next to his office which he occasionally used for welcoming female visitors. Tonight it was ready for her arrival: a dish piled high with sweetmeats and biscuits stood on a little table, a bottle of champagne sat in an ice-bucket and incense burned in one corner of the room. Glancing round, the girl noticed that a crucifix and two small objects on the walls – perhaps pictures of saints or photographs of dead relatives – had been draped with handkerchiefs to prevent their witnessing the Honourable Member's human frailty. This seemed to confirm her mental image of Palizzolo as a devout little fellow, boring rather than dangerous. She sat down by the pastries – in her present circumstances and surroundings the only source of comfort – and, while The Swan satiated both himself and her with conversation, proceeded almost single-handedly to empty the dish down to the very last sweetmeat and biscuit. The champagne, too, helped her feel better: at peace with herself and the world. For the first time after months of privation, she felt the sense of sleepy wellbeing that comes with a full stomach spread through her limbs, and decided that if vice produced this sort of feeling, it was immensely preferable to virtue.

When Palizzolo eventually undressed and climbed on top of her, Filicetta had to stop herself laughing, because the little man, who was as pink and round as a suckling pig, clamped himself onto her nipples and wanted to be breast-fed, held on her lap – even spanked . . . The girl's biggest worry about this appointment with a stranger had been that she might feel revolted when he touched her, but in the event she felt nothing at all. On a full stomach she would be able to let anyone touch her – that was how she felt that first time, at any rate. In the end The Swan fell asleep sucking on one of her nipples. The next morning he gave her a hundred lire and another appointment for the following Saturday evening. He told her that her breasts were brighter than the Milky Way and asked – or rather ordered – her not to mention their meeting to anybody at all.

From that day onwards, Palizzolo had not been able to wean himself off Filicetta's breasts. The rest had followed naturally in the course of just one summer – the flat with the pot of basil and the bird cage; the silk dresses, the hats, the bags and the Parisian underwear which cost twenty-five or even thirty lire a piece and was sold in only one shop in Palermo – maybe even in the whole of Sicily. (The Swan was a devotee of women's lingerie and Filicetta had no objection, since he was paying.) The Honourable Member had one other peculiarity that the girl became aware of when he began reciting poems which he said he'd written especially for her, but which were quite incomprehensible, so crammed were they with words nobody ever uses. But Heaven help you if you looked bored or irritated. Palizzolo was an implacable poet, and Filicetta had to listen to his gibberish with a show of great enthusiasm, otherwise he'd go into a sulk and not reappear for days. However, apart from the verse and his obsession with sucking women's nipples, he seemed to be an entirely innocuous creature who wouldn't hurt a fly. He was always very kind to Filicetta. He gave her money every time he visited and even brought small presents: a picture of the Madonna del Carmelo in a silver frame, a box of silk handkerchiefs, a plate of sweetmeats . . .

This, therefore, had been the first turning point in Filicetta's life. And then, one October evening in 1894 – the year in which she had become a different person – The Swan, after leaving a hundred lire on her kitchen table, announced that he would no longer be able to support her; not on his own, at any rate. He explained that his parliamentary duties required him to live in Rome for part of the year. During his absences Filicetta would have to get used to receiving other men: a few good friends of his, who would identify themselves at her door with the words "The Honourable Member sent me", and would treat her with as much respect and generosity as he did, because Palizzolo's friends were all men of honour . . . As the Swan spoke, Filicetta was thinking how her status was about to alter again, from kept woman to prostitute, and she felt afraid.

"What kind of people will I be mixing with?" she asked herself. "What's going to happen to me?" But if she pulled back now that she'd gone this far, she'd lose everything: her home, Palizzolo's protection, her comfortable life . . .

"Naturally, I'll be visiting too when I'm in Palermo," The Swan continued. "In fact, at those times I want you exclusively at my disposal. I don't mean to share you with anybody and if I'm allowing other men to visit you while I'm away it's only for your own good, because otherwise you'd run out of money or get bored and end up being unfaithful to me anyway."

Before leaving he repeated, yet again, the same stuff he always came out with: the stories he used in his poems, about priestesses of Love in ancient times who guarded the sacred flame; about her breasts that shone brighter than the moon and stars; about Circe the witch who turned men into pigs; about nymphs and satyrs and Frine, who dazzled the Judges with her naked body . . .

The new customers began to show up. Her regular clientele consisted of a former Member of Parliament, a stockbroker, two lawyers, one of The Swan's brothers, a businessman and two taciturn men about whom Filicetta could only have said that they were men of honour, that is members of the

Mafia. Then there were the occasional strangers who would knock on her door during the night and give the password:

"The Honourable Member sent me."

It was with them that Filicetta had become a real whore, and she had been amazed at how natural and easy the transition had felt. It reminded her of something she had overheard a few years previously, concerning a Marineo girl who had run off to Palermo to live with a pimp: "Some women have whoring in their blood."

She couldn't get those words out of her mind. "It must be true," she thought, "that some women are born whores. If it isn't, how can I live so contentedly, without any guilt? If I'm a whore out of pure necessity, how come I sometimes feel pleasure with my clients?"

She attended Mass on her own every Sunday, in the church of San Niccolò. She also went regularly to confession and communion, because she considered such things to be akin to physical cleanliness – hygiene of the soul. But no matter how often she promised her confessor that she would change her way of life, she knew she wouldn't, just as she knew he would go on forgiving her every time she confessed. What were priests for if not for forgiving people's sins? Sometimes she felt as if she were two people: the respectable young mother of two she used to be and the strumpet she was now; other times she felt quite convinced that her present identity was the real one and that everything she'd done before coming to Palermo had only happened because, although she had whoring in her blood, there had been no outlet for it in Marineo.

She liked Palermo. She liked feeling enveloped by that gentle and mysterious city, so vulgar and raucous in some areas, so opulent and silent in others ... She liked sitting outside the Messinese ice-cream parlour on the Marina, showing herself off to the *donninnari* – young men on the lookout for a wife – and other Jack the Lads who were no longer young nor single, but spent a large proportion of their useless time in search of a love affair they hardly ever found. She liked watching the picturesque equipages of the nobility drive by, and listening to the common people whisper the names of the carriages' owners – under their breath, because you can't go shouting that kind of thing on the street; you have to be discreet.

"Did you see who that was?" husbands would murmur to their wives, and young men to their *zite*. "That was the Conte di Toledo ..." Or "That was the Principe di Trabia, the Duchessa di Pietratagliata, the Principe di Mirto ..."

She liked strolling down the Càssaro on winter mornings or in the spring when the sun is not yet hot enough to redden the skin, window-shopping or watching the passers-by. On summer evenings she liked to hire a carriage and drive out of town to the Quattro Canti di Campagna, or even further, to the Santa Rosalia sanctuary on Mount Pellegrino. She had made friends with her dressmaker, a young woman who had left her husband to become the mistress of a prince. Every Sunday they would go to the Favorita racecourse to watch the prince's horses. After a while however, the nobleman sent the two women a message, politely requesting them to stay away from the races – their presence had been noted and might cause gossip. So the two friends had started going to the baths at Acquasanta and to the "Saturdays at the Flora", to admire the Villa Giulia illuminations and watch the puppet shows along the park walks ...

Filicetta even had a suitor: a tall, thin, red-haired student called Antonio who in his native Girgenti (as she had only very recently discovered) was engaged to marry one of Crispi's greatnieces – Angela, the very one who, in 1894, had picked *ciuri de maju* for herself and for His Excellency's daughter. In Palermo, Antonio shared lodgings in Via dei Biscottari with two university friends, in the same building that housed Filicetta. He had become taken with the idea of seducing her, although he knew perfectly well, as everybody did, that she was the mistress of Palizzolo and his mafioso friends and that fooling around with her would be playing with fire . . . Far from frightening him, the danger excited him. Whatever the cost, he kept telling himself as he studied for his final exams, he had to inveigle his way into Filicetta's bed before returning to Girgenti. So he declared his love to her when they met on the stairs; he showered her with billets-doux and poems which made her laugh ("Who'd have thought," she murmured to herself as she read them, "when I was still a peasant girl at home, that I'd turn into the sort of woman who inspires poetry") and left flowers on her doorstep, picked behind the park-keepers' backs as he returned from university. In his efforts to overcome the resistance of his beautiful neighbour, he had even gone so far as to propose marriage. Filicetta was surprised.

"He must be very naïve if he doesn't know what I do for a living," she thought to herself. Then it occurred to her that even this was just another ruse to get her into bed. She asked her friend the seamstress to make some discreet inquiries about this young man who was so in love with her, and in that way discovered the truth: as soon as he got his degree, the handsome Antonio would at long last be joined in holy matrimony with a young lady from a good Girgenti family, one of Crispi's greatnieces . . .

In Palermo, Filicetta was almost happy. She lived life one day at a time; her health was good and, after the amnesty for those involved in the *Fasci* revolt, she no longer had to fear persecution for what had happened to her in her home town. In time, even the memory of her children caused her no pain. Saro and Nuzzu, the girl reasoned, were born to be peasants. Nobody could change her sons' destiny any more than they could change hers. Her past life, she thought, was over for good.

But when, an hour earlier, she had opened the front door to

a stranger and come face to face with Don Piddu *Facci di lignu*, her past had descended on her with a thunderous roar and the two Filicettas who had been living as strangers within her – the peasant girl of long ago and the woman of today – found themselves clutching each other in a terrified embrace, or perhaps, for a moment, became one person again.

"The Honourable Member sent me," Don Piddu repeated, then, since Filicetta gave no reply, but just stood staring at him wide-eyed, he made as if to push past her into the flat. It was then that she brought her hands to her head and started to scream: "Help! Help!" so loudly that the neighbours came out to see what was wrong. "Go away!" she yelled.

Although *Facci di lignu* remained impassive, he was surprised and embarrassed by Filicetta's welcome. He couldn't remember ever having seen this girl before. He wondered who she was, and came to the conclusion that she must be the widow or daughter of one of his many victims – which victim was not important. Better find another woman . . .

"All right, all right," he said. "I'm going," but then seized her by the arms and looked her in the eye with an expression that made her feel faint. "I'm going," he repeated, "but if you start screaming again while I'm on the stairs I'll come back up and wring your neck like a chicken."

He turned his back on her and looked over the banisters. All the neighbours who had come out onto the landings promptly retreated into their homes and the sound of closing doors echoed from every floor. When silence finally returned to the deserted stairwell, Don Piddu walked down at a leisurely pace, whistling a song that was all the rage in Palermo. He reached the front door and disappeared.

2

Palermo, 28 April 1897

The streets and squares of Palermo were still filled with sunshine and people; the shops were all still open. In Dottor Salvo's pharmacy a few idlers were discussing the day's news in the paper. They had split into two factions: those in favour of Crispi called it shameful to drag the former Prime Minister, now nearly eighty, into the affair of the missing Bank of Naples money. The authorities should just throw the Managing Director, Commendator Favilla, into gaol and put a stop to all this mud-slinging at a man like His Excellency, one of the creators of Italy. The opposing faction held that His Excellency was the great corruptor of Italian politics, a man who over the previous twenty years had pocketed millions of lire from the banks of Rome, Sicily and Naples. He should be rushed into the dock before he died, to show him to the world in his true colours. This second faction, so drastic and pitiless in its proposals, actually had only two members: the brothers Onofrio and Salvatore Curreri, purveyors of bonbonnières and novelty items, who had never made any secret of their radical, not to say anarchist, tendencies.

Paolo Costanzo, the assistant pharmacist, whom everybody respectfully addressed as "Dottore", had avoided getting involved in the discussion. He wasn't particularly interested, and in any case he would not have had time to stay until the end. When the grandfather clock struck seven he removed his white coat, exchanged a few quiet words with the owner,

Signora Ignazia Salvo, and left the shop. He set off on foot along the Càssaro, responding to acquaintances' calls with a wave of his hand or a glance which said "Sorry, I'm in a hurry!" He turned into Via Maqueda, then Via Sant'Agostino (which, at the time of our story, had not yet become what it is today: a sort of *souk* selling cheap jewellery, cloth and household items) and finally entered a three-storey house which boasted a coat of arms over its front door.

This house which, according to the sign by the door, should have been called "Palazzo Villarosa" was known to older locals as "Casa Palizzolo", and had a history which interweaves with that of The Swan's family and can be summed up in a few lines while Dottor Costanzo talks to the doorman. It was bought around the middle of the century by the brothers Pietro and Eugenio Palizzolo, two *liuni* from Caccamo who, having made their fortunes in their home town, took it into their heads to become noblemen too, and moved to Palermo in the hope of achieving this ambition. The Palizzolo family's slow advance on the Sicilian aristocracy began there, in the Via Sant'Agostino mansion, but many obstacles presented themselves along the way, particularly at the start, when the best idea the two provincial tyrants could come up with was to add the maiden name of their mother, Concettina Nobile, to their own, and to begin signing themselves Palizzolo de'Nobili. Above the door of Casa Palizzolo there appeared a coat of arms that would never have been found in a heraldic manual – a purely fictional device with a tower, conceived and produced expressly for the new Nobili family by a marble carver in Via Sant'Antonino. The aristocracy – the real one – did not bat an eyelid, but the whole affair ended after only a few months, because a nephew of Concettina's (also called Nobile) became an infamous bandit and filled the newspapers with accounts of his crimes, and with his surname. Thus disgraced, the Nobili family had disappeared, but the crest above the entrance to Casa Palizzolo remained in place, because in the meantime the two *liuni* had managed to acquire a title – that of *"Cavaliere"*, which, since it is not authentically aristocratic, can be accompanied by any coat of arms.

Some time later Cavalier Eugenio, The Swan's uncle, died of a heart attack and Cavalier Pietro, his father, decided to earn his promotion to the upper echelons of society by offering his services to the King. It was 1866, the year of the Palermo revolt and the cholera epidemic. Pietro Palizzolo had a pamphlet printed ("A faithful Account of the Conditions and Needs afflicting the labouring Classes of Sicily, or: On the general Calamity of Her Peoples"), which was dedicated to the King and the members of the National Parliament and was, in effect, his candidature to the governorship of Sicily. The pamphlet – destined to become the laughing stock of half of Italy and all of Palermo – contained some vivid descriptions of the ills besetting Sicily ("Recoil, dear reader, recoil in horror! Each day new cases of suicide present themselves! One father, upon witnessing his beloved little ones prostrated at his feet begging for bread – bread to sustain the Breath of Life within them, doth exclaim at such a pitiful request: 'Ah, hard earth, wilt thou not open up before me?'"), as well as Cavalier Palizzolo's plans for those areas of the economy and public life he intended to run in person, if appointed. He would set everything to rights single-handedly: agriculture, the banks, the railways, ecclesiastical wealth, pensions, prices . . . Only one area of government – that of Public Health – would Pietro Palizzolo have delegated. He claimed that his private doctor, Cataldo Cavallaro, had found a cure for cholera and must immediately ("with electric speed") be put in a position to save thousands of lives. ("He discovered an antidote to gastric fever which on the third day did cease. I was struck down with it, together with my son, but a smiling Cavallaro with mathematical precision confirmed its cessation on the third day.")

Cavalier Palizzolo's pamphlet – its most important sections printed in Gothic type – was delivered to the King by one of his Palermo attendants and posted to every Member of Parliament and all the newspapers, but produced no result of any kind. Parliament did not convene to discuss it, neither did His Majesty summon the author to grant him that governorship of Sicily whose first and obvious consequence would be the conferral of a title such as Count or even Prince . . . Nobody, in Italy or anywhere else, appeared to have noticed Pietro Palizzolo's proposal. The aspiring Governor, embittered, was already contemplating a second pamphlet which would forcefully reiterate the ideas in the first and denounce the conspiracy of silence surrounding it, when he fell ill with cholera and died, at only fifty-nine, in spite of Dottor Cavallaro's antidote. He did not even live to attend his daughter Irene's marriage to a penniless (but genuine) nobleman, as a result of which the house in Via Sant'Agostino finally acquired a suitably aristocratic name: "Palazzo Villarosa". Nor did he see the impoverished fellow's coat of arms, also authentic, replace the Nobili tower above the doorway . . .

But it is time for us to return to our pharmacist. After announcing his arrival to *Zu* Tano the doorman, Dottor Costanzo climbed three flights of stairs and rang the bell by a door which bore the inscription "The Honourable Raffaele Palizzolo, Member of His Majesty's Italian Parliament". He was expecting to be shown in immediately, because the time and date of their meeting had been agreed some days previously and because the matter he had come to discuss was of concern to pharmacists – a profession which (at least in Sicily) was respected and courted by politicians of all parties. The maid, however, informed him that the Honourable Member was occupied with other visitors and politely requested Dottor Costanzo to wait a few minutes.

Alone in the antechamber, Costanzo noticed that the door to

The Swan's study was ajar and that the room beyond was empty. Our pharmacist, aware of his host's habits, guessed that the meeting the maid had mentioned was probably taking place in the vicinity of the lavatory. He shook his head and smiled. One of the things The Swan was known for in Palermo was this quirk of compelling his guests, particularly those he called "friends" ("Pay no attention to me! We're friends! Don't let's stand on ceremony!"), to talk to him through a door, from the other side of which came gushing and plopping noises that did not always harmonise with the gravity of the matter on which the politician's intervention was being sought. Dottor Costanzo had had his own experience of this a couple of years previously, when Palizzolo welcomed him into his bedroom at nine in the morning wearing a hairnet and moustache-extender which made him look more like a seal or a small walrus than a human being. The Honourable Member then leapt out of bed in his underpants and made his way to the toilet, urging his guest to carry on talking, whatever might happen on the other side of the door.

"I'll be listening all the same," he had said . . .

The pharmacist was still standing by the door to The Swan's study when he heard footsteps on the other side and the agitated voices of people discussing something which seemed to worry them deeply.

"So," he thought to himself, "the meeting has adjourned from the bog to the Honourable Member's study." He stepped back out of sight and listened intently. Much of the conversation coming through the door was incomprehensible, but from those words which did get through intact he gathered that The Swan and his guests were discussing a crime story which had been back in the papers over the previous few weeks, after years of absence and neglect: the Notarbartolo affair! Hardly a day went by in Palermo without the *Giornale di Sicilia* vendors shouting to the Quattro Canti di Città new and sensational

76

revelations about this murder, which still managed to excite public interest because of the way it had remained unpunished and shrouded in mystery. The Honourable Palizzolo had once again been mentioned as the man behind the crime but, more importantly, the actual killer had been named in black and white for the first time: Don Piddu Fontana.

This was appetising stuff, so the pharmacist – after checking he was alone and could not be seen from the front entrance – placed his ear against the door. He heard the Honourable Member whisper: "Even if they do arrest Don Piddu, nothing will come of it, because he's got all the evidence he needs to prove he was in Tunisia at the time . . ." All Costanzo could understand of the next few words was the name of Senator Codronchi Angeli, who had been sent to Sicily as provisional administrator following the repression of the *Fasci*, and the word "scum". He also heard: "Double-crossing" and: "they're mistaken".

"Don't worry," said an authoritative voice which the pharmacist had never heard before. "There's no evidence against him, and there never will be . . . As long as we're at Police Headquarters, anything that turns up will be binned . . . only traitors' gossip . . . so much hot air . . ."

". . . to begin all over again," said another unknown voice. "Someone is grassing . . . Leave him to us . . ."

"Yes, yes," soothed the previous speaker. "We mustn't make a big thing out of it."

There followed more unintelligible sentences from the other two, then Costanzo heard the Honourable Member again.

"So far everything has gone perfectly . . . even Lucchesi . . ." (Michele Lucchesi was Chief of Police in Palermo). "You'll get your arrears from the railway company . . . we're already pay-ing you the interest . . . have a bit of patience, for Chrissakes!"

At this point a new person joined the conversation. He had a low, rasping voice which, after a slight hesitation, Costanzo recognised beyond any possible doubt. It was Giuseppe Carollo, the railway inspector who, at the time of the first investigation, had been suspected of being the murderer or at least an accomplice. For years Dottor Costanzo had worked in a pharmacy in Via Sant'Antonino, almost opposite the railway station, where Carollo had been one of his most regular customers, partly because he was constantly unwell – or thought he was – and partly because that particular pharmacy had become a meeting place for off-duty railway staff in Palermo. After his spell in prison the inspector had moved to Catania and Costanzo hadn't seen him again, but his voice was very distinctive and the pharmacist knew it almost at once.

"But I'm telling you they're serious this time," Carollo whimpered. "They need a conviction . . . political reasons . . . myself and Garufi, the brakeman . . . life imprisonment . . . I'm afraid." There was a brief silence, then he went on: "Let me show you, look, here . . . and here . . . in Catania they beat me for the first time . . . going back to prison . . . cover for friends . . . I've already spent more than a year inside . . ." Costanzo could hear that he had started crying. "They'll give me life . . . six children . . ."

"Here are two thousand lire, my friend." This was The Swan's voice again; he was speaking louder so as to sound reassuring. "For Heaven's sake! Haven't we just explained you can rest easy at night? . . . There's a senior police officer here with us; I'm a Member of Parliament; we've got endless resources, friends everywhere . . ." After a few less audible sentences, The Swan raised his voice again. "Go back to Catania," he told the railwayman, "and trust us, whatever happens. You heard what the Inspector said while I was on the toilet: the police haven't got a shred of evidence, not even a witness. All they're doing is trying to scare you into confessing. They're the same old tactics. You know them better than I do; after all, you've been through it once already!"

Costanzo heard the sound of chairs being pulled back and footsteps heading in his direction. He only just managed to move away from the door before it opened wide and the Honourable Member appeared, one hand on Carollo's shoulder. He spotted the pharmacist and said:

"I won't be a moment. I'll just say goodbye to my friends then I'll be with you." On the doorstep, as The Swan kissed his guests on both cheeks, the railwayman seized the chance to whisper in his ear:

"That man ... Dottor Costanzo – he knows me! He may have heard us!" Palizzolo tutted in vexation and murmured: "Tell the doorman." Then he turned with a smile to the pharmacists' representative and waved him towards his study: "Please, do come in."

The conversation between pharmacist and politician was brief and totally unproductive, partly because both men had other things on their minds ("Should I tell the police what I've seen and heard?" Costanzo was asking himself. "What'll happen to me if I do?"), and partly because Palizzolo, though he had occasionally championed some of the trade's interests in the past, did not have to rely on pharmacists at election time. He had other methods for procuring votes – much more effective than a pill-merchant's advice!

Having obtained a promise, as formal as it was vague, that The Swan would lobby for a special clause on Sicily in the forthcoming pharmacies' legislation, Costanzo found himself back on the stairs, then in the street, mulling over what he had seen and heard. He'd only taken a few steps, however, when his path was blocked by a short, stocky young man – a *picciotto* – who had his shirtsleeves rolled up above his elbows and an unlit cigar-stub in his mouth. The youth, whose face was perfectly square and not much more expressive than a kneecap, asked for a light, then, on the pretext that there was too much wind, shoved Costanzo against the corner of a house, and held the tip of a nine-inch knife against his stomach.

"Who are you?" the young man asked. "What's your name?"

Terrified, Costanzo looked around, but realized that even if he called for help nobody would come to his aid: passers-by averted their eyes; a woman who had been standing a few yards away in her shop doorway stepped hastily back inside, the moment the *picciotto* pulled his knife. Life went on, the pharmacist thought; and would go on, even after his death!

"My name is Paolo Costanzo . . ." he stammered. "I'm a pharmacist. My wallet's in the inside pocket of my jacket – take it. Take my watch too, only please don't hurt me!"

"What were you doing in the Honourable Member's house?" the young man asked, eyeing him as a butcher eyes a quarter of beef before cutting it up to be sold.

Costanzo gave up hope. "This is it," he thought. "One of Palizzolo's mafiosi must have spotted me listening to his boss and sent this killer to silence me . . . Heavenly Father, I'm in your hands. Please save me!"

"I had to ask him a favour," he explained humbly. "Not for myself, but for pharmacists in general. There's a bill being discussed in Parliament . . ."

The *picciotto* grimaced impatiently and cut him short: "Was anybody else there? Who did you recognise?"

"I didn't see anyone . . ." poor Costanzo stuttered. "I don't know anything . . . Please let me go . . ." In one lightning movement the knife was at his throat.

"Who did you recognise?" the young man repeated.

The pharmacist tried again: "Nobody . . ." but he felt the tip of the knife pierce his flesh. He began to cry.

"Only one man . . ." he sobbed, "I didn't know any of the others . . . I swear it . . ."

"The railwayman?" the *picciotto* asked.

"Yes, sir . . . just the railwayman . . . he used to be a customer . . ."

The pressure on the blade increased. Costanzo felt the warmth of blood – his own – running down his neck and under his shirt, and all he could think was: "Jesus save me". At this point the assassin brought his wide, low forehead very close to the pharmacist's, until they almost touched.

"Talk and you're dead," he whispered in a cavernous voice. "Mind your own business." He removed the knife from Costanzo's throat, lit the cigar-stub with his victim's matches, pocketed them, and disappeared as suddenly as he'd arrived.

Our pharmacist's first impulse, once he became aware that he was alone, was to escape, but when he tried to move his legs he realized they weren't able to support him, and that he would fall over if he left the wall. So he stayed where he was, staring in amazement at the handkerchief soaked in his own blood and at the people going about their business, passing him by as if he were invisible: the lamplighter, housewives with shopping bags, shopkeepers taking in their wares and closing their shutters. Everything around him was calm and normal; there was a profound sweetness in the dusk of that clear spring day, and in the expressions of the people who looked straight through him, almost with affection. For the first time in his life, Dottor Costanzo became aware of his infinite solitude as a man and as a Sicilian, and felt crushed.

A newspaper vendor in Via Maqueda was yelling like a madman:

"Latest on the Notarbartolo affair! Astonishing new leads! Bartolani the superwitness arrives in Palermo!" but Costanzo wasn't listening. He just stood there holding his handkerchief to the wound in his throat and repeating to himself:

"It was nothing. Nothing happened. I'm still alive!"

3

Palermo, 16 May 1897

The 9.50 stopping service from Messina drew in to Palermo's central station almost half an hour late, as usual. A single passenger got out of the first-class carriage in the middle of the train: a man of about forty, of medium height and sturdy build, who looked around with a weary and anxious expression, then followed the rest of the passengers towards the ticket hall.

This man – who might have felt less troubled if he'd known that the novel he was walking through was not his own, and that he was merely a bit-player in our story – was Salvatore Diletti, Stationmaster at Messina. In his pocket was a telegram from the management of Sicilian Railways summoning him to Palermo on this train "to receive an extremely urgent communication". Ever since it had arrived the previous morning, poor Salvatore had been deeply anxious. At least a thousand times he'd asked himself why they should want to talk to him: a transfer? Promotion? A reprimand? An envious colleague making Heaven knows what accusations? He had tossed and turned all night, allowing neither himself nor his wife to get any rest, and still had not found an answer. The more he thought about it, the less likely it seemed that there could be anything to warrant such an urgent summons – and on a Sunday as well! He had got up before five to catch the train, and now that he was finally in Palermo he wanted only one thing: a quick solution to the mystery. He walked briskly to the end of the platform, but was stopped at the entrance to the ticket hall by two police officers conducting identity checks. As soon as they heard his name they ordered him to follow them. So – thought Salvatore Diletti – they'd been posted there specially to wait for him. He turned pale.

"What do you want?" he stuttered. "Are you sure you're not making a mistake? I haven't done anything!"

One of the officers tried to reassure him. "Don't worry," he said, as if those words would be enough to calm the poor man. "You're not in trouble. We just need you to help us with an inquiry."

"Inquiry? What are you talking about . . . ? I've only just got off the train." The terrified stationmaster didn't have a clue what was happening. Might there be a direct link, he asked himself, between these policemen and his summons to Palermo? Or were the two things separate, simply part of some terrible curse which had been invoked the previous day and might possibly go on for ever? When was it going to end? He tried to get the officers to see reason.

"Please," he said, "let me go! I'm the stationmaster at Messina. This is my identity card. This is a telegram from my superiors. Do you want me to get the sack? I'm here on duty!"

"Come with us," ordered the officer who hadn't spoken yet. With an irritable shrug Diletti gave up arguing and followed the policemen without a word, assuming that they would be taking him to the local police station. But when they reached Via Sant'Antonino (now Via Lincoln) the policemen instructed Diletti to get into a large black carriage which which was parked on the corner.

"Dottor Lucchesi, the Chief of Police, wants to talk to you," they told him.

The stationmaster felt he must be in a dream – the kind of nightmare you long to wake up from but can't . . . Seeing he had no choice, he obeyed. Inside, he found himself sitting next to a portly, almost completely bald gentleman, who proffered a fat, sweaty hand and said:

"Don't be alarmed, Diletti. I'm Palermo's Chief of Police. I do apologise for asking the railway management to summon you instead of doing it myself, but I'm sure you appreciate that, if I'd gone through the usual procedures, news of our meeting would have been public at once and the press would have been on your back before I got a chance to speak to you . . . I'm afraid I've put you through some anxious moments, but it couldn't be avoided."

"Please tell me what all this is about," the stationmaster implored, close to tears. "What am I accused of? I've never neglected my duties. I've never broken the law! Believe me!"

Lucchesi looked at the man sitting next to him and realized he was petrified.

"In Heaven's name, calm down . . ." he laughed. "Don't be afraid. No charges or complaints have been made against you; none at all." He nodded to the coachman, who had turned round to receive instructions, and the carriage set off towards Via Maqueda while he carried on explaining.

"You, Diletti," the Chief of Police told the unfortunate stationmaster, who was staring at him intently, anxious finally to make sense of what was happening to him, "are the only person who has seen the face of a man . . . a man who may be the killer of poor Notarbartolo, do you remember? Your statement at the time gave a very detailed description, which the magistrates and I have read many times in the past few months . . ."

Diletti's eyes widened: now he understood! He looked at Lucchesi and felt tempted to say:

"You damned cop . . . I made myself sick with worry for a day and a night because of you . . . when the police stopped me at the station I nearly had a stroke!" But his relief that neither the police nor the Sicilian Railways were after him was so great that he almost forgot what he'd been through.

"So," he thought to himself, "it's the murder on the train that made this bastard play his dirty trick with the telegram, and had me rushing to Palermo." He remembered reading in the paper a few days before that the police had reopened the Notarbartolo investigation and arrested three people: the two railway-men who were held for questioning during the first inquiry, and a third man, one Giuseppe Fontana from Villabate, who was suspected of being the actual murderer. He, Diletti, was acquainted with Carollo the ticket inspector and Garufi the brakeman from his days at Termini Imerese station. He knew Carollo to be a very low-ranking mafioso who would never have been entrusted with any murder, let alone the murder of someone as important as Marchese Notarbartolo. Fontana, on the other hand, he knew nothing about, but when he read his description in the paper, it reawakened memories of that February evening four years before, when he'd waved off the Palermo train, then stood on the platform watching the carriages pass until there appeared – standing at the window of the leading compartment in the first-class carriage – a man with a grim and resolute expression, whose eyes had looked through Diletti for a moment before he disappeared with the train ... Four years on, the stationmaster could still remember that unknown passenger's face, the determination in his eyes; when he read in the paper that Giuseppe Fontana, arrested for the murder of the Marchese Notarbartolo, was also known as *Facci di lignu*, it occurred to him that such a nickname would suit the man in the first-class compartment.

The carriage drove along Via Maqueda to the Quattro Canti, turned into the Càssaro, which was thronged with men, women and children out in their Sunday best, and headed in the direction of La Cala.

"I need your help," Lucchesi told the stationmaster. "I've arrested a man and I think he's Notarbartolo's murderer. I have one statement and some circumstantial evidence to use against him, but no firm proof that would allow me to keep him in gaol. Things would be different if we could establish that he was the man you saw on the Palermo train, in the same compartment as the victim, on the evening of the first of February 1893 – the man you described so well in your statement to the police. By the way: do you reckon you could still identify that fellow on the train, after four years?"

"Yes," the stationmaster replied without the slightest hesitation. "You don't see many faces like that, thank God! And having to describe him to the police at the time printed it on my memory like a photograph." Suddenly he realized he had said too much, and the harassed look returned to his face. "Whoever he is, this man you've got in prison, I don't want anything to do with him," he almost shouted at the Chief of Police. "I don't want to see him. I did my duty four years ago – I told the police everything I knew. What else do you want from me?" He seized the policeman's hand. "Please, Chief Inspector," he implored, "have a heart. Tell them to take me back to the railway station. My family in Messina will be worrying. I have to let them know I'm all right. I don't know anything!"

The carriage was nearing Ucciardone prison. Lucchesi looked at the man sitting next to him; probably the only person in the world capable of ensuring the conviction of the assassin or assassins of Commendator Notarbartolo: the witness the whole police case rested on.

"There you are . . ." he thought to himself. "I get called the Mafia's Inspector because I've never sent a senior mafioso down; because I try to coexist and make deals with them . . . But what on earth can I do in a city like Palermo, where not even the widows of murder victims will collaborate with the police; where a policeman on the beat can't even get passers-by to tell him the name of Mount Pellegrino? Every now and again you come across someone like this Diletti: a rare bird, an honest man who comes forward to tell us what he's seen and gives us a vital piece of information, a key which could unlock the whole investigation on its own. But it never unlocks anything, because in the whole of Sicily you won't find a single person prepared to stand up and testify against a mafioso or point him out in an identity parade. Even the most upright of upright men will lie, retract, deny all the evidence, swallow nails and glass to feign insanity . . ."

He sighed. "I'm going to make sure you can see our man without being seen," he told the stationmaster, "and you're going to tell me if he really is the fierce-looking individual you saw on the train. I have to be certain, you see. This is not a trivial matter; it could mean a life sentence."

Diletti was racked with anxiety. "I know, I know," he kept repeating. "But if the prisoner does turn out to be the man I saw at Termini Imerese, the whole thing will get in the papers. There's no avoiding that! Everyone will know I was the one who identified him and my life won't be worth twopence."

"Nobody knows you're here today," the Chief of Police countered, "and nobody'll ever find out what you're going to say to me in a few minutes' time, in private, between prison walls. I give you my word of honour that this whole business will be treated with the utmost discretion. You've seen for yourself how secretly we called you here . . ."

The carriage passed through the gates of Ucciardone into a courtyard where they were met by the prison governor and a number of warders, who escorted the newcomers to a corridor with doors along both sides. To observe the prisoners in their cells, you had to look through spyholes embedded in each door. Lucchesi asked the stationmaster to see if he recognised anyone and told him to take it slowly. "The prisoners can't possibly know who's outside – you don't run the slightest risk."

Followed by the police chief and the governor, Diletti began to uncover the spyholes one by one and put his eye to them.

Almost all the prisoners were half naked and sat, or lay, doing nothing, on their bunks, although he did see one calmly masturbating and another writing or doodling in a notebook.

At the fourteenth or fifteenth cell, just as the stationmaster was beginning to tire of this game, he saw a man standing with his back to him, beneath the vent that let air and light into the cell. When he heard the spyhole cover being lifted, the man turned round and Diletti, confronted with Don Piddu *Facci di lignu*, started with surprise and fear. He dropped the spyhole lid, took a step back and looked with a dazed expression at the two officials, who were following his every move.

"It's him!" he said.

"Are you absolutely sure, Diletti?" Lucchesi asked in a honeyed tone. "You've only seen him once before, very briefly, four years ago. Please go back and have another careful look. Impressions don't count in this sort of thing, you know, only certainties . . ."

Overcoming his reluctance, the stationmaster uncovered the spyhole again. Don Piddu, sensing that he was being watched, looked towards the door with the same expression he'd had on the evening of the crime. The witness stepped back.

"It's him," he said. "Without a shadow of a doubt. His hair's a bit greyer than I remember and he seems to have put on a bit of weight, but that's definitely the man I saw at Termini Imerese on the first of February 1893, in the first-class carriage of the Palermo train!"

Lucchesi was pleased. A glimmer of light at last, where only recently he'd been utterly in the dark. But he knew his problems weren't over. In a sense they were only just beginning. He looked the stationmaster in the eye.

"I hope you realize, Diletti," he said gravely, "that what you've just said is too important to remain between the two of us. We must inform the Crown Prosecutor. So now we're going to go to the courthouse where Dottor Cosenza is waiting to hear the outcome of this identification, and you will kindly tell him everything you told me, without adding or omitting anything. It's your duty."

The stationmaster had been counting on being allowed to return to Messina immediately. Lucchesi's words stunned him.

"Chief Inspector," he stuttered, once he regained the power of speech. "You promised me . . . it was a trap . . . I've only just realized. Oh God, my children!" The thought of his children – destined to be orphans if he, Salvatore Diletti, dishonoured himself by testifying against Don Piddu Fontana – brought tears to his eyes.

"Please don't hand me over to those murderers," he implored, weeping. "Have pity on my family. I'm an honest man! Do you want me to get killed for your Justice? Are you looking for a martyr?" He sobbed like a child and blew his nose loudly on a big linen handkerchief, but Lucchesi didn't soften.

"Don't make such a fuss, Diletti," he said severely. "Be a man! I'm warning you: if you refuse to come to the courthouse and sign a statement about this morning's events, you'll be an accomplice in a murder case and I'll keep you locked up in the same wing of the Ucciardone as the man you identified, until you've lost your job and your reputation. I mean it: you have been warned."

The prison governor accompanied the two men out through all the gates and sentry posts, and they got back into the Chief of Police's carriage. On the way to the Palace of Justice the station-master's state of mind was that of a man suddenly afflicted by some terrible catastrophe, or even one who has been condemned to the scaffold. He kept up a continuous lamentation: "Holy Father what a day . . . a plot . . . in a murder case . . . Jesus help me . . ." and dabbed at his forehead and eyes with a handker-chief. Lucchesi, on the other hand, stared straight ahead without letting his expression betray his thoughts, or uttering a word throughout the journey.

When they reached the Palace of Justice, the Chief of Police took his victim by the arm and marched him up the wide staircase to the first floor, then on into Dottor Cosenza's office. The Crown Prosecutor was a slight, bald man with gold-rimmed glasses, who kept smiling and repeating: "Good, good . . ." for no apparent reason. Lucchesi told him about the identification and about having had to threaten his witness with arrest when – after pointing out Piddu Fontana promptly and unhesitatingly from dozens of prisoners – Diletti had proved reluctant to identify the suspect formally by signing a statement.

Still smiling, Cosenza looked at the stationmaster, who suddenly leapt from his chair and began hitting his head against the wall so hard that it made the whole room echo, yelling between blows:

"Damn this head of mine! Damn me! It's all my fault!" The Chief of Police and the Prosecutor tried to restrain him – the latter, to be honest, verbally rather than physically – but he thrashed about like a madman and could only be immobilised and returned to his chair once they were joined by the two security men assigned to their floor. The witness had now turned purple and was croaking: "My heart . . . I'm dying . . . it hurts . . . oh God . . . the children . . ."

"Calm down," Cosenza told him. "What are you getting so worked up about? All you have to do is tell us what you saw and whom you recognised, then we'll let you go home . . ."

"A little signature at the end of a statement, what does that cost you? Then it'll all be over . . ."

On hearing the words "signature" and "statement", the dying man began to roll his eyes and struggle in his chair again, shouting like a man possessed:

"Nothing! I saw nothing! Can't you get it into your thick skulls I didn't see a bloody thing? I made it all up. All I saw that evening in Termini was the ruin of myself and my family! I saw nothing and I'm signing nothing! Nothing! Nothing!"

"I can't see what there is to be afraid of, Diletti," the Crown Prosecutor coaxed. "If you talk, that man and his accomplices will go to gaol and you'll be safe and sound at home, with a clear conscience. Why can't you see that?"

The stationmaster's lips drew back into a sardonic grin, and his wild eyes fastened on Cosenza.

"How many people are you planning to arrest?" he asked. "A hundred, a thousand, a hundred thousand? And how long do you think you're going to keep them in gaol?" The lawyer made no reply, so Diletti answered his own question. "The more people you arrest and convict, the sooner I'll be dead. No, I'm sorry gentlemen, you have to realize that I know nothing and saw nobody, either today or four years ago. I made it all up then, as I made it all up this morning! I don't know why – perhaps to seem important, or to please the people questioning me . . . The truth is I'm an idiot: yes, sir, a bloody idiot! . . . I don't mind giving you *that* in writing! If someone asks me what I've seen, I tell them, even if I saw nothing at all! I say: I saw a man, he looked like this or like that, he was leaning out of the window of the train . . . but that's only because I'm mad!"

He was sobbing and pounding his brow as he spoke. Cosenza peered at Lucchesi over his gold-rimmed lenses, with a look that said: "What are we going to do?"

Lucchesi set his jaw and raised his voice.

"That's enough!" he ordered. "We're tired of your whining and hysterics. Now we're going to draw up a nice little statement confirming that you saw and recognised the man on the train, and you're going to si . . ." He broke off half way through the word, because Diletti was no longer there. With a sudden dart, the stationmaster had managed to get through the door to the stairs, leaving everyone in the room dumbfounded – Prosecutor, Chief of Police and the security men who should have held him back but didn't have time to move a muscle.

The first to recover from the shock was Lucchesi, who shouted at the guards:

"What are you waiting for? Get him back!"

Meanwhile Diletti had already got to the entrance hall and was running towards the doorway without a thought in his head except escaping as fast and as far away as possible.

Left alone with the Chief of Police, Cosenza turned to him and shook his head with that exasperating smile of his which at times – Lucchesi thought – made one want to slap him . . .

"Good, good," the Prosecutor observed. "He's got away." He leant back in his chair. "Shall I tell you," he asked, still smiling, "how this identification business is going to end? Tomorrow I'll send Stationmaster Salvatore Diletti a summons to attend an official identity parade with Giuseppe Fontana di Vincenzo, remand prisoner in Palermo's royal penitentiary. He will come, because he can't disobey a legal summons. He will look straight at the man he recognised so unequivocally today and declare that he's never seen him before in his life." He lifted a hand, as if to intercept Lucchesi's objection in mid-air. "Yes, I know, we could charge him with obstructing the course of justice and put him in the cooler for a week or two to get him to change his mind. But he wouldn't. It's been a waste of time . . ."

Lucchesi shrugged irritably. "If you only knew how little I care about the stationmaster, Fontana or any of the Mafia's victims!" he told the magistrate. "I wish there were more of them. Killers, victims – they're all in it together . . . The only thing that matters to any of them is keeping the police out of their affairs. As for the Notarbartolo inquiry," he added after a brief pause, "I swear on my honour to give a month's salary to anyone who'll take this cross off my back. Trying to gaol a murderer four years after the crime in Sicily is like trying to empty the sea with a teaspoon. But the press, damn and blast it, has taken this business up again and the heavy guns in Rome are bombarding me with telegrams and commands. They want the investigation concluded within the week; they want the trial to start before the summer . . . As if I could do anything about it! As if I were personally holding up the inquiry! I'm doing everything humanly possible, you've seen that. But I'm not the Almighty and I can't work miracles, and I don't have any way of frightening these bastard witnesses more than the Mafia has done already . . ."

4

Milan, 5 December 1899

"Hey, you, *terún*!* You're not in the Grand Hotel you know. Time to get moving!"

The attendant at the Hostel for the Destitute, nicknamed Cerberus, yanked away the two numbered blankets he had issued to Salvatore Cancilli the previous evening and woke him out of a beautiful dream – one of those dreams which, while not quite equal to a real night of passion with a woman, can nevertheless act as something of a substitute. Abruptly returned to the reality of a public dormitory in Milan on a winter's morning, the Sicilian railed against his tormentor: "*Mannaia lu cunnutu! Vaffangulu!*" (Bloody cuckold! Sod off!) He lowered his legs over the edge of his bunk and cast another resentful glance at the hostel attendant, who was continuing his circuit of the large room, flinging aside other sleepers' blankets as he went. He rubbed his temples with his fists and went on: "*Chi mi ti spúnnanu, cunnutu! Jetta sangu!*" (Rot in hell, you cuckold! Bleed to death!)

He closed his eyes for one last glimpse of the unknown Milanese woman who, a moment before, had been lying naked and warm in his arms, making love to him so passionately that he forgot his four sons, his Sicilian wife and even the initial stages of his dream. Where had he met this obliging young

---

* *"Terrone"* (*"terún"* in Milanese dialect) is a term of abuse used by Northern Italians to signify "Southerner". It comes from the word *"terra"* (earth) and has connotations of "country bumpkin" or "yokel". [Translator's note]

woman? He managed to bring her back into focus. She was small, blonde, and rippling with movement . . . But just as the girl rematerialised next to Salvatore on his bunk, he was woken by a shove and Cerberus' voice exploded in his ears again:

"What are you doing, *terún*? Sleeping upright?"

Looking around, he realized that it really was late, and all the other Sicilians had left. Only a handful of down-and-outs remained among the empty bunks: a few *barbún*, as the Milanese called their tramps, and a couple of ugly-looking characters from the city's underworld, who answered Cerberus' invitation by calling him a bastard and a *struns mal cagà* (ill-shat turd) and threatening to wait outside for him with a knife . . . Salvatore stood up on slightly wobbly legs and went to the cloakroom to retrieve his coat and jacket. As he struggled into these vastly oversized woollen garments he remembered his first few days in Milan, after his journey up from Sicily in a third-class carriage packed with other poor wretches who'd been summoned, as he had, to testify in a pointless trial . . . In those first few days – Salvatore remembered – the alleyways around the Palace of Justice had filled with short, dark men wearing peasant's caps and women wrapped in the long black shawls which hid part of their faces. As they walked past, you could hear the rustle of the newspaper and cardboard they had lined their clothes with, so as not to freeze. They all slept in hostels, convents or station waiting rooms, and one or two had even ended up in hospital with pneumonia or incipient hypothermia. Then the Milanese newspapers had noticed their presence and the self-interested charity of the Northern Italians had reached out to them.

One Sunday morning Salvatore Cancilli, numb with cold, had been walking along a street lined with shops and eating places, when a large man in a white apron had beckoned at him from one of the restaurant doorways and asked:

"Are you one of the Sicilians who've come up for the

Notarbartolo trial?" He felt Salvatore's jacket to judge its thickness, then dragged him inside. He called to his wife and daughter:

"Terisina! Ghitta! Come and look at this poor *terún* who's wandering round Milan with next to nothing on, in this weather! He's like a block of ice! Get him my coat – the old one. I won't be wearing it again anyway. And a woollen vest. And some socks. Have a good look in the bottom of the wardrobe – there should be a scarf too, and a pair of gloves."

In no time at all the restaurant filled with people: chefs, kitchen porters and the owners and assistants from neighbouring shops, all eager to get a look at the *terún* who, the large man explained, had come to Milan "because where he lives there's a criminal organisation called the Mafia which controls everything, even the courts, so if the Mafia kills somebody down there, they have to have the trial here in Milan, otherwise they might as well not bother."

"Tell the truth! Be a good witness!" he exhorted his *terún*, who was burning with shame and anger at hearing his beloved Sicily insulted in that way. ("What Mafia?" he muttered to himself. "It's all lies.") He even tried to refuse the large man's charity – he didn't want to get undressed there, in front of the women, or put on stuff which, apart from anything else, was too big for him. But the large man insisted, yelling incomprehensibly in Milanese dialect: "*Ten a ment, terún, che Milan gh'a'l coeur in man!*" (Remember, *terún*, that Milan has a kind heart!), so that in the end he had to comply. He changed from head to toe into his benefactor's castoffs, feeling more and more ridiculous, then went out into the street, where he realized that even Milan didn't seem all that bad when one was wearing a coat, and that those warm clothes were bringing back his will to live.

As he walked on he met other Sicilians, bundled up as he was in ill-fitting woollen clothes, who explained what was going on.

The Milanese papers had published stories about their plight and people had been moved to pity. Some readers were offering accommodation; others, when they saw them on the street, called them over to give them coats, scarves, gloves and woollen underwear. In Via Larga, at the offices of the Cooperative Association, a special canteen had been set up for the Sicilians, where Milanese women cooked them the food they were accustomed to and a whole meal cost only ten centesimi!

Well fed and warm at last, the male witnesses took to spending most of their time hanging around the girls on the fruit stalls in Verziere Market, or the nannies walking children in the Castello gardens. All of them, without exception, thought of only one thing: the women of Milan, and they told each other amazing tales about love affairs they claimed had happened without their even trying, but which somehow never seemed to happen to poor Salvatore.

"How is it possible," our Sicilian Railways employee asked himself yet again on that morning of 5 December 1899, as he walked down the steps of the hostel, "that I'm the only person I know who hasn't had an affair with a Milanese woman yet? Am I that much denser than the others?"

The clock on the corner of Via Brera stood at ten past seven. It was still dark, but the city was already filled with traffic and noise. The pavements were crowded with people hurrying to work, running for the tram, or stopping off for a coffee in bars which, at that hour, still had chairs piled up on the tables and sawdust on the floor ... If it hadn't been so cold and flat, Salvatore thought as he set off towards the Courthouse, Milan could even have been beautiful. The streets were clean and tidy, the houses as large as the grandest palaces in Palermo, and the walls plastered from top to bottom with advertisements promoting things like Nubiani shoe-polish ("No need for a brush"), or Hunyadi Jànos mineral water ("The finest of purgatives"), or Ischirogeno ("Restores vitality"), or Fernet Branca

("With regular use – digest even stones"), or Iperbiotina Malesci ("Reinvigorates and prolongs life"), or Rituali hand- and chest-warmers, highly commended at the 1892 Exhibition . . .

Never before had Salvatore Cancilli seen so many advertisements, so many shop windows, so many goods for sale, so many electric lightbulbs, or so many women out on the streets, going about their business as if they'd been men – and since he always stared and tried to say something to all of them, he was in constant danger of being run over by a tram or a carriage. At times he would actually freeze, like a dog who has spotted a hare, and lie in wait for one of those young housemaids or seamstresses who dressed in a way which seemed calculated to drive men wild, with high heels and little overcoats so tight one could easily imagine what lay underneath. Those young women who used clothes like a second skin must, Salvatore reasoned, have much looser morals than their Sicilian counterparts, and therefore did not have to be respected. They were *boddane* (whores) who must be castigated, and every time he came across one of them, Salvatore would step into her path and stare at her with such wild eyes that the hussy really ought to have been inspired, if not to repent, then at least to reflect upon her sins . . . But so far, in spite of being *boddane,* none of these housemaids and seamstresses had shown any interest in our Sicilian's crusade, and so it was this morning. A couple of girls simply sidestepped him, while a third hit him with the handle of her umbrella, shouting: *"terùn"* and *"foera di ball"* (piss off). There was even one, close to Piazza Scala, who said:

"Go to hell, you ugly runt! Have you ever looked in the mirror? You've got a face like a cabbage stalk!"

Near the Caffè Marini in Piazza Scala, the men selling the *Corriere della Sera* and the *Secolo* were rushing between customers, a bundle of papers under their right arm. Occasionally they would shout out a headline, such as "The four scandals of the Notarbartolo trial!"; "No proceedings against Palizzolo!"; "Fontana said to be in hiding in Villabate!"; "Stop press! – Musolino the brigand at the gates of Cosenza". Most passers-by, too cold and pressed for time, simply handed a coin to the vendor and took their paper without even stopping, but there were a fair number of others, both men and women, who crowded round the single pages hung up on pieces of string, commenting on the news with remarks like "Never seen anything like it. What's the world coming to?"

Salvatore went over to read the headlines, as he had every morning since he arrived in Milan. He was interested in the exploits of Musolino the brigand and the international news, particularly from America. The Notarbartolo trial, on the other hand, was a matter of complete indifference to him, because he believed it would all fizzle out and, in any case, it had nothing to do with him. He was just a minor witness, one of the railwaymen who'd been called over by their colleague Giuseppe Sanfilippo when he stumbled over a body on the tracks between Altavilla and Trabia, that was later revealed to be that of Commendator Notarbartolo. Salvatore had seen a dead man on the ground, nothing more; he considered it not just strange, but at a level of insanity entirely worthy of the contorted minds of Northerners, that he should be forced to travel all the way up to Milan and stay there for weeks, or possibly months, waiting for the Clerk of the Court to summon him, and for the judge to ask him one question, to which he could offer precious little in reply. He knew the two defendants, Carollo and Garufi, who were railwaymen like him, and he was positive they had not killed Notarbartolo. It was a matter of what you might call job demarcation. Murderers, Salvatore believed, have neither the time nor the need to work on the railways, and railwaymen would never be brave enough to stand in for a murderer. If you want to grow old in Sicily, you have to know your place. Nonetheless, he saw nothing unusual in Carollo and Garufi being tried for a crime they hadn't committed – they'd be acquitted anyway, and everyone knew that in this sort of trial the real culprits were rarely charged.

In other words, it was business as usual, and would have remained that way if an event had not occurred during one of the first court hearings – an event which in Palermo would have attracted about as much attention as a fart in a church, but here in Milan caused an uproar, an explosion of popular indignation which the newspapers amplified like a sound box. Naval Lieutenant Leopoldo Notarbartolo, the victim's son, had told the judges he knew for certain that his father had been killed by the mafioso Giuseppe Fontana, on the orders of the Honourable Raffaele Palizzolo; the national press had pounced on this piece of information and the so-called Mafia theory. Hardly a day went by without newsvendors in every square in Italy shouting fresh headlines from a trial which fascinated all respectable people and kept the whole nation on tenterhooks. Newsboys yelled that Palizzolo had resigned his seat; that Fontana the mafioso had fled abroad; that Palizzolo's resignation had been retracted; that Giuseppe Fontana was in hiding in Sicily, sheltered by powerful friends; that someone in the Palermo police force had deliberately misdirected the initial inquiries . . .

The citizens of Milan were stunned. All over the city people were discussing Sicily and the Mafia. Everyone agreed that the time had come to *nettà l'ort in cà di terùn, dagh na bela ramassada* (clean up the Southerner's home, give it a good sweep-out), that they were sick of hearing about banditry and Mafia, that villains like Palizzolo should be in prison, not in Parliament. Salvatore listened to these comments in almost incomprehensible Milanese dialect, and felt there was something strange and morbid about the interest Northerners were taking in things which did not concern them; things which had been like this since the world began. What did the Milanese know about the Mafia? What right did they have to talk about it? The Mafia is like God – it is everything or nothing and, like God the Father, does not want you to speak its name.

This morning, as he stood in Piazza Scala looking at the newspapers, Salvatore again reflected that nothing could be more foolish than this obsession for uncovering the truth which seemed to have seized not just the judges, but the whole of Milan.

"The truth!" our witness said out loud, as he hurried along the Galleria towards the Palace of Justice. "The truth!" he repeated. "Who," he wondered, "is supposed to benefit from this truth they're seeking in the courts? – The judges? The murder victims? The newspapers?"

He turned into an alley. "These stupid Milanese," he went on, noticing a girl in a cherry-red coat approaching in the distance, "would do better to stop fretting over other people's truth and pay more attention to their own. They're already so numbed by the cold that, to get their attention, their women have to flaunt everything they should be hiding – bums, tits, legs . . ." He bumped into the girl on purpose. "Hello, gorgeous! I could eat you like a cherry! Listen, I've got something to tell you!"

The courtyard of the Palace of Justice in Piazza Beccaria was crammed with Sicilians: *Zu*, *cummari* and a few *don*s, busy commiserating with each other and exchanging news of distant relatives as they waited for the Clerk of the Court to come and read out the list of witnesses to be heard that day.

A man everybody called Don Rosario was pondering, out loud, the existence of the Mafia. "I'll give a hundred lire – no, a thousand," he bellowed, "to anyone who can explain, once and for all, what this famous Mafia is. The first time I heard it mentioned was in Milan!" *Zu* and *picciotti* stood around listening and nodding. A few even exclaimed: "You're absolutely right!" and Don Rosario warmed to his subject. "Is it something you can touch?" he asked himself and his listeners, rolling his eyes and waving his hands about; "Something you can eat? Something you could run into on the street? Is it made like water – like air?"

Fascinating questions; but Salvatore knew that nobody there was going to enlighten Don Rosario on the Mafia, so he moved on. At the centre of the next group was another defence witness, one Totò Tartamella, who spent most of his time frequenting the Milanese brothels and always had some new story to tell. That morning Don Totò was enthusing about a woman in the house on Via Pantano who, he said, went by the name of Elvira, but was in fact a certain Maria Rosaria from the province of Siracusa ("one of us"), as sensual and fiery as only Sicilian women can be. An elderly man, who looked none too healthy and was wearing such an oversized coat that his hands were hidden by the sleeves, scolded Don Totò for wasting his money, but the speaker laughed in his face:

"Nonsense! I spend my money on practical remedies, and you'd be well advised to follow my example." He explained to his listeners that *boddane* were his medicine. Thanks to them, at the age of fifty-seven, he still ate, slept and shat like a young man. He lifted a finger at his audience.

"Take my advice," he exhorted them. "A good course of *boddane*, if you can afford it, keeps you in better shape than a month taking the waters."

When the Clerk of the Court appeared on the stairway, silence fell immediately. From his pocket, he produced a piece of paper which had been folded into four. He opened it out, placed a pair of reading glasses on his nose and began to call out a list of names, lowering his head after each one to peer over his lenses and check if the person was coming forward.

"Giuseppe Sanfilippo," he read, "Santa Sorge, Salvatore Piazza, Candeloro Mangiò, Giuseppe Romano, Salvatore Cancilli . . ."

"Here!" Salvatore said, and made for the stairs. As he climbed them, he reflected sadly that his stay in Milan was over without his having managed a single affair with any of the women he'd seen about the streets, swaying their hips as they walked, snugly enveloped in their coats. In two days' time he'd be back in Palermo, reunited with his wife Carmela, his four children, his relatives, his colleagues . . .

The Court of Assizes was crowded. In the front rows, opposite the judges' high-backed chairs, sat the lawyers, divided into three groups. The press benches were full, and in the public gallery every available seat was occupied by wealthy Milanese ladies and gentlemen, who were passing the time before the start of the hearing by reading the paper or discussing the progress of the trial.

Salvatore looked around and saw the latest arrivals from Sicily – the men in caps, the women wrapped in their too thin, too black shawls – queuing for their free *Corriere della Sera* meal-tickets. He saw Judge Rossignoli, the presiding magistrate – a small man with blue eyes and reddish hair – busy counting out the vouchers. Next to him, another robed official (possibly the Public Prosecutor) was chatting with two lawyers. On the other side of the hall, beyond the *carabinieri* in full-dress uniform, was the cage which held the defendants, Carollo and Garufi. Salvatore Cancilli felt honour-bound to go over and greet them, but was not prepared for the welcome he received. Garufi was sitting in a corner of the cage, staring vacantly. His lawyers had told him not to talk to the witnesses, so when Salvatore addressed him he simply lifted his chin and clicked his tongue against the roof of his mouth – quite a common gesture in Sicily, which can signify, depending on context, "I've got nothing to say to you", "I don't know you", "I don't give a toss about you", and many other things besides.

Carollo was standing up, gripping the bars of the cage with both hands and staring at Judge Rossignoli. He didn't even notice Salvatore calling him. The railway inspector had the look of an invalid: he had lost weight, his complexion had changed from olive to greenish, his eyes shone with fever and his lips were drained of almost all their colour. From the very first day of the trial the papers had portrayed him as a dissembler and a hypocrite, busy pretending he was at death's door, and inventing all sorts of petty excuses to hinder the judges' work. To prove to the world that he was in earnest, Carollo was now preparing to die as befitted his chosen character, at only forty-two, surrounded by the indifference and hilarity of the public.

"Your honour!" Carollo cried out in a voice so deep and hoarse it already seemed to come from beyond the grave. "I have to make an important statement. A very important statement! I want it to be taken down."

The journalists flocked to the cage but Judge Rossignoli, who was blessed with the gift of imperturbability, went on handing out vouchers without paying the slightest attention to the defendant's words or what was going on around him.

"I'm as innocent as Jesus Christ!" Carollo shouted at him. "Like Christ I have worn the crown of thorns; like him I am a saint. My father's name was Santo and I, whom you are about to crucify, am a worthy son of that Santo among saints! You who persecute me, you lawyers and policemen, you judges – you will come to kneel at my graveside! You will weep and beat your breast, but it will be too late."

Silence had fallen in the hall, broken only by an occasional titter from the lawyers or the public and the voice of Judge Rossignoli checking over the list of the previous days' vouchers with the Clerk of the Court.

"What sort of justice is this, which keeps me in prison? What have I done?" Carollo yelled, clutching the bars of his cage and turning eyes that shone with fever towards a wooden crucifix on the wall above the judges' heads. "Who are those who will judge me? And," he asked the journalists standing in front of him, "who are you?" He looked at them in amazement, as if this were the first time he'd ever set eyes on creatures with two legs and two arms, in woollen overcoats.

"What is this place you've brought me to? *Where am I?*"
Nearly everybody in Milan's Court of Assizes was now laughing openly. At the back of the hall there was even a brief round
of applause, and a "Bravo!" of the sort used to encourage actors
in the theatre. But Carollo was undaunted.

"All these events are incomprehensible to me," he observed,
then turned back to Rossignoli. "I stand here before you like
a shadow, but many eyes will weep after my death and many
tears be shed – by your children too – to atone for this just
man's blood. Remember!"

There was a second burst of applause, much louder and
longer than the first, and some of the audience requested the
whole soliloquy over again ("Encore!"). Carollo, however,
simply crossed himself and went to sit down at the back of
the cage with his face to the wall. The Clerk went up to
Judge Rossignoli, who had just finished distributing the food
vouchers and, pointing at Carollo, whispered in his ear:

"Should I record the fact that the defendant addressed the
court before the hearing and made a threat against the judges?"

Without even looking up, Rossignoli made a movement with
his left hand, as if waving a fly from his nose. With his right he
picked up the bell on the desk in front of him and rang it several
times, declaring: "Let the hearing begin."

5

Palermo, 8 December 1899

Lit by the dim glow of a gas-lamp draped with cloth so as not to dazzle the invalid, the bedroom of the Honourable Raffaele Palizzolo, hung with his images of saints and devotional objects (crucifixes, scapulars, Sacred Hearts, consecrated pendants and olive sprigs), was at the centre of a melodrama which had been on show at the Via Sant'Agostino house for several days now and whose title could have been "The Agony of The Swan".

At seven o'clock in the evening on Friday 8 December, almost the full cast was on stage to rehearse the closing scene. To the right of the leading man's bed sat his unmarried sisters Concettina and Cecchina, round and pink like sows in skirts, wearing starched bonnets on their curly hair and clutching rosary beads tightly between their fingers. Standing to the left were Antonio and Eugenio, his brothers, and his eternal fiancée Matilde, who was talking in whispers with The Swan's other sister, the Duchessa Irene di Villarosa. The character who had just made an exit was the Duca di Villarosa – a little man, known in the Palermo society of the day as "His Vacuity", because of his haughtiness, his frivolity and the inanities he uttered every time he opened his mouth. Another brother, Captain Gandolfo Palizzolo (nicknamed "Captain Trouble" because of his weakness for duels) was pacing back and forth between the well-lit study and the dying man's dim bedroom. And as he paced he muttered, snorted, and made furious and threatening gestures, as if he wanted to fight the entire universe but had not quite decided whom to challenge first.

The Honourable Member's study, next door to his bedroom, was also part of the set. Avvocato Bordonali, a lawyer and the administrator of the Palizzolo family land and possessions, was sitting on the chair where, in health, The Swan had rested his own pale buttocks. He was talking quietly with Avvocato Raffaele Scherma, the nephew of another *avvocato*, Lucio Scherma, who had been on the board of directors of the Bank of Sicily with Palizzolo in Notarbartolo's day. Standing to their right was Matteo Filippello, *curatolo* of the Villabate lands, who was looking around at the lawyers and all the other visitors as if he couldn't believe what he was seeing.

"Is it really possible," his eyes seemed to say, "that a great man like Palizzolo, a man beyond reach, can be thrown to the fury of the crowd without even having done anything really bad – just a routine murder six years ago?"

Also present were Salvatore Geraci and Tanino Scandurra, two *picciotti* awaiting orders which never came, because by now nobody knew the number or the whereabouts of the Honourable Palizzolo's enemies, or if the siege could still be broken. The enemy was everywhere. The premonition of imminent catastrophe hovered in those two rooms like a nightmare, and seemed to render futile both the rantings of the swordsman Gandolfo (accustomed to arbitration by the blade), and all the strategies, offensive and defensive, being discussed by the lawyers. The place felt like a fort which is about to fall to the enemy but refuses to surrender. The captain of the garrison, fatally wounded, was lying in bed with an ice pack on his head, occasionally emitting heart-rending moans such as "Ouch!" and "Ahh!" which moved all present to deep pity.

"How he is suffering, poor thing," murmured the Duchessa di Villarosa, while Matilde turned away so as not to let her fiancé see her tears and the porcine sisters ran the beads of the rosary faster and faster between their fingers. "How can they torment a human being so? And what about our friends in Rome? Where are they when we need them? What are they waiting for?"

The Swan, lying on his bed of pain, was also thinking of his friends – it was precisely this searing thought which forced him to open his eyes from time to time, part his lips and faintly murmur:

"Irene, Concettina, Cecchina, please . . . send someone to the telegraph office to see if anything's arrived for Matilde from the Honourable Gattorno or the Honourable Gallo . . . My telegrams are being intercepted by the police, we know that, but my friends in Rome have Matilde's address as well as mine – they'll get in touch with her . . . We can't just sit here doing nothing, suspended in this agony . . ."

On these occasions Matilde would approach the bed to stroke the dying man's forehead.

"Don't fret, my poor dear," she said. "We've thought of everything. One of our men is at the telegraph office – the moment a cable arrives he'll bring it here. But in the meantime you mustn't worry. You know what they say: no news is good news . . ."

"This is agony, agony . . ." The Swan croaked feebly as his eyelids gradually closed, only to open again suddenly as he snarled: "They'll pay for this. By God they'll pay for this. I know who they are!"

"Calm down," Matilde would plead. "Don't upset yourself like this. We're all here beside you, you can see that, and when the time is right your friends will contact you. Don't be impatient."

Don Raffaele had taken to his bed at around eleven o'clock that same morning, when *Zu* Tano, the doorman, came upstairs to tell him that the house was surrounded by plainclothes policemen and that Don Nicola Cacace – the "king" of the

Capo area who knew every cop in Palermo – had counted more than ten in Piazza degli Aragonesi, Via Sant'Agostino and Vicolo San Marco alone. But The Swan's "death agony", as he called it, had really begun towards the middle of November, when the judges at the Milan Assizes had called Lieutenant Leopoldo Notarbartolo to the witness stand, and when that unmentionable worm, that traitor, chose not to behave like every other relative of a Mafia victim and shocked the world by accusing him, the Honourable Raffaele Palizzolo, of having ordered the mafioso Piddu Fontana to kill his father. All hell broke loose. The Socialists, who in Milan behaved as if they owned the city, flocked to the story like crows to a carcass and published whole pages on it in their hysterical newspapers. But who would have thought – The Swan asked himself, anxiously twisting the tips of his moustache – that the case against Don Piddu and himself would have spread from young Notarbartolo's ravings and the columns of marginal Socialist news-sheets to the so-called independent papers: the *Secolo*, the *Corriere della Sera*, the *Stampa*, the *Messagero*, the *Nazione* and even the *Giornale di Sicilia*? And nobody with any sense would ever have believed it possible that a man so widely feared and revered as himself – a *Commendatore*, a member of His Majesty's Parliament – could find himself facing such a lynching overnight, without the slightest gesture of solidarity from those who, only days before, had shared power with him in Palermo.

Caught unawares, Palizzolo had tried to defend himself by claiming to be the victim of a conspiracy aimed at undermining not just him, but Crispi and the whole of Sicily. At this first attempt, however, he failed in his efforts to create a smoke-screen large and dense enough to hide everyone and everything. From Naples, His Excellency Francesco Crispi let the news-paper editors know that Palizzolo's affairs were no concern of his, and that the Honourable Member, innocent or guilty, should sort the matter out with the judges. As for Sicily, the most widely read and respected daily on the island attacked Palizzolo as determinedly as the Northern papers, and with the same lines of argument, accusing him of being the head of the criminal organisation known as the Mafia – the existence of which was thus unequivocally acknowledged by Sicilians for the first time.

"It's a passing storm," The Swan said to himself. "Editors need a constant supply of stories to keep their readers interested – something as stale as the Notarbartolo case won't be of use to them for more than a few days."

But as it turned out, the country's outrage grew and acquired a new resonance which had nothing to do with the public's normal fascination with murder. There was much more than curiosity behind the wave of indignation which made honest Italians from the foothills of the Alps to the island of Sicily shake with fury, and Palizzolo had realized this one morning at the end of November when, having been scheduled to talk to the Chamber of Deputies on behalf of the Sicilian sumach industry, he had not managed to get beyond his first sentence. Yells, whistles and abuse drowned his voice out from the very beginning, however much the Vice-President of the Assembly rang his bell and pleaded "Honourable colleagues! Silence, please!"

From every part of the semicircle of seats, voices called out:

"Tell us about the Mafia! Tell us about the Bank of Sicily! We want to know why Notarbartolo died!"

Since Palizzolo carried on talking about sumach, the Socialist members began to chant: "Notarbartolo! Notarbartolo! Notarbartolo!", clapping their hands and thumping the benches, and in next to no time every deputy in the room, from extreme left to extreme right, had joined in the chorus.

The situation was unprecedented: the chamber in Montecitorio was turned into a circle of Hell as, for three or four long minutes, the whole of the Italian Parliament clapped and chanted the dead man's name:

"Notarbartolo! Notarbartolo! Notarbartolo!"

The Swan returned to Palermo. He spent his first evening with Filicetta, sucking her nipples and whining on about how the whole world was against him; how he was the Italian Dreyfus, and how the Socialists wanted him dead, until the woman fell asleep and started snoring. Over the following few days he began to mix with influential people again – in the Town Hall and at the Casino and Unione clubs . . . but everywhere he went he was met with grim expressions and sealed lips. When he tried to visit several people at home, they instructed their servants to tell him they were out.

He barricaded himself in his Via Sant'Agostino headquarters, confining himself to study, toilet and bedroom, surrounded by relatives and friends who brought regular dispatches from the city and the telegraph office. But when a Sicilian politician in Rome sent him a telegram announcing that Parliament was about to authorise criminal proceedings against him, Palizzolo attempted one last desperate sortie. He went to the Palace of Justice to ask the advice of the Public Prosecutor, Vincenzo Cosenza, a gentleman and friend of the Friends. What should he do? Cosenza simply looked at him, smiling as always, and uttered a few evasive words, chief among which were "good, good" and "patience". The Swan had himself driven to the Prefecture, where he was received by a junior official instead of the City Prefect, and where he finally realized that his situation was desperate.

Once more he shut himself up in his house, with his family and an ever-shrinking inner circle, to await news from Rome which never arrived. So it had continued until just before eleven o'clock that morning, when *Zu* Tano had come upstairs to say that the house was surrounded by police, and The Swan had undressed and taken to his bed, saying in a feeble voice that he felt ill. He had pains almost everywhere: heart, kidneys, liver, intestines, spleen, head . . .

The doorbell rang and Matilde left the room. When she returned a few minutes later she went over to the bed and placed her hand on the invalid's forehead. He opened his eyes and looked at her questioningly.

"Nunzio Puleo's here," Matilde said. "He's in the entrance hall. Do you want to talk to him or shall I tell you what he told me?"

Nunzio Puleo was one of Matteo Filippello's men – a *picciotto* from Villabate who worked as doorman in the Prefecture. "Why didn't he come sooner?" breathed the dying man. "What does he know?"

"He says he couldn't leave the office during working hours without somebody noticing," Matilde replied. "Everybody there is in a state of high excitement, as if something big were about to happen at any moment. Apparently the Interior Ministry in Rome keeps sending coded telegrams and the Marchese De Seta deciphers them personally, without letting even his secretary see them. Three of them came just this afternoon."

The Swan closed his eyes again: "Ouch."

"Do you want me to bring him in here?" Matilde asked. "Or shall I tell him he can go? I don't think he knows anything else." There was no reply, so Matilde went back to the entrance hall to dismiss the young man. It was a few minutes past eight and one of The Swan's unmarried sisters whispered in his ear:

"It's Concettina! I'm going to the kitchen now to make you two eggs and a little broth, but first you must promise on our dear mother's soul that you'll eat something. How can you stand up to your enemies on an empty stomach?"

"You're so thin and pale, you look like a ghost," said the other spinster, Cecchina. "You've got to fight back!" she urged him. "You've got to pull yourself together! An important man like you – *Cavaliere*, *Commendatore*, Member of Parliament – can't just give in to a handful of scoundrels, even stop eating because of them!"

"There are millions of them, not a handful," The Swan wheezed, bringing his hands to his temples, which must have been hurting badly, "and they want me dead . . . Oh God, my poor head!"

Concettina began to cry. All of a sudden the raised voices of two or more men were heard on the staircase. The Honourable Member gave a start, opened his eyes wide, removed his hands from his temples and sat up in bed.

"What's happening?" he asked. "Who's in the house?"

The voices approached rapidly. One of them belonged to *Zu* Tano, who was shouting:

"The Honourable Member is ill; he can't see you – how many times do I have tell you?"

The other voice – the one that was replying: "Whatever his state of health, we've got to see him, so get out of my way" – was not entirely unknown to Don Raffaele either, but he would not have been able to place it, had the person in question not burst into his room, followed by the doorman and Matilde. It was Francesco Ronca, the Police Commissioner.

"He's come to arrest me," thought The Swan, who had known the man for many years and even recommended him for promotion. "Maybe not," was his next thought. "He's on his own . . ." But then a second outsider invaded the half-light of the invalid's bedroom – a tall, stout man who had taken a little longer than the others to climb the stairs. He introduced himself from the doorway.

"Chief Inspector Stroili," he said. "Palermo Police Force."

There was a moment's silence, broken only by the sobs of the porcine sisters.

"Can't you see I'm ill?" asked The Swan in a faint, unsteady voice. "Who authorised you to barge into my house uninvited at this time of night?"

"Please may we have some light?" Stroili asked The Swan's brothers. Eugenio Palizzolo removed the cloth from the gas-lamp and it was as if a theatre-hand had switched on the stage and auditorium lights half way through the last act of a melodrama, while the hero was still in his final agony, surrounded by a wailing chorus. The Swan's family blinked at each other in that light, too strong and too white for their performance, then turned to the intruders. What were those policemen *doing* in their house? Who did they think they could scare with these bullying tactics?

Inspector Stroili went over to The Swan's bed. "I have to ask you to get up at once and accompany us to the police station," he said. Then, realizing he was being too abrupt, he tried to soften at least the tone of his summons, since its meaning was, under the circumstances, glaringly obvious. "The Chief of Police, Cavalier Sangiorgi, wants to discuss some extremely urgent matters with you," he explained.

The sick man stared at the inspector for a long time, as if unable to understand his meaning and trying to glean it from his expression. Then he removed the ice pack, which made him look ridiculous. With a sob in his voice, he inquired: "Am I being arrested?"

Stroili opened his arms wide and nodded. "Yes."

"Has Parliament authorised this?"

Again the inspector nodded: "It has."

The Swan clutched at his heart and let himself fall back on the pillows, gasping and rolling his eyes upwards until the whites showed.

"Oh God . . ." he sighed. "A doctor . . ."

His brother Antonio, who was the nearest to the door, rushed out to seek medical help. The porcine sisters by his bed began to wail, emitting blood-curdling shrieks which were shrill enough to damage the eardrums and be heard at the other end of the street. Eugenio Palizzolo, his face wet with tears, hurled himself at the policemen and shouted, pointing at the expiring Swan:

"How can you think of moving him, in that state? Do you want to kill him? Is that what you really want?"

"Do you feel no pity at all? What sort of men are you?"

"Shame on you!" shouted Artillery Captain Gandolfo Palizzolo, "Captain Trouble". His cheeks were dry, but his lower lip and chin were trembling convulsively. He advanced threateningly on Inspector Stroili and lifted a hand as if to strike him, while his other hand felt the stripes on the collar of his jacket.

"If you weren't a policeman," he warned, "and I wasn't wearing this uniform, I'd make you regret coming into this house without being invited by my brothers! Get out, while you can still do it on your own two feet!"

Inspector Stroili took a step back. "Gentlemen," he announced to Gandolfo, Eugenio and everyone else in The Swan's bedroom and study. "I warn you that down in the street I have enough reinforcements to carry out my duty whatever the circumstances, and arrest anyone who obstructs me."

After a moment of tense silence, the dying man's eyes rolled back to their normal position and his voice rasped:

"Gandolfo, Eugenio, don't be foolish . . . He's right." The Swan managed to sit back up in bed by lifting himself onto his pillows with his elbows. He turned to his porcine sisters:

"Shut up, please! You can do your keening when I'm dead. These gentlemen," he said, pointing the policemen out to his relatives, "can't be blamed for what's happening. They're honest men doing their duty . . ."

Inspector Stroili couldn't wait to get out of this madhouse and be shot of the whole affair. "Can you walk?" he asked The Swan, adding quickly: "If you can't, we'll take you in an ambulance. I'm sorry, but that's the law."

"I'm feeling better," The Swan murmured. "I'm feeling better now." He waved his sisters away, pulled back the blankets, threw his legs over the edge of the bed and stood up, in his underpants and woollen vest. He swayed unsteadily on his feet so that Eugenio had to help him walk. When he got to the middle of the room he stopped.

"I am innocent," he said, "and the Law will acknowledge it. No honest citizen could possibly believe I am guilty. Nobody who knows me and has seen what I've done – what I can still do – for my city, would want to see me in prison!" He turned to Inspector Stroili. "Tell me," he asked, "do you think I am guilty or innocent? Speak your mind!"

"It's not for me to say," the inspector replied. "I've been ordered to arrest you and that is why I'm here. The rest has nothing to do with me."

The Swan nodded as if the inspector had said he thought him innocent. "And Cavalier Sangiorgi," he went on, "does he think I am guilty?"

Inspector Stroili was an experienced and patient officer – the most patient officer in the Palermo force – but this situation was beginning to get on his nerves. This man in his underpants, standing among his relatives with a dazed expression on his face and no apparent intention to get dressed, would have tried the patience of a saint.

"What do I know? Ask him yourself in a few minutes, time!" he let slip, then recovered his politeness. "Sir," he requested, "please be kind enough to get dressed and ask one of your relatives to find you a pair of pyjamas for your first night in Ucciardone. Sheets and all the rest can be dealt with tomorrow morning. Someone can bring them to the prison, where they will be inspected and passed on to you."

"Do you think they'll send me to Milan?" asked Palizzolo. "Whatever happens," he explained hurriedly, seeing the inspector's glare, "I will insist on being judged by my fellow Sicilians, because the plot against me is above all a plot against the city of Palermo and the whole of Sicily! I will call on every Sicilian to defend me . . ."

"God Almighty!" Stroili blasphemed. "Will you or will you not get it into your head that you're supposed to get dressed? Otherwise I'll have you removed bodily, as you are, in your underpants. Do you want to keep me chatting here all night? I give you one more minute. God Almighty!"

Paradise (1901–1904)

I

Naples, 6 August 1901

His Excellency spent his days seated at his window staring out at the sky of Naples. If from time to time he lowered his gaze to his knees and hands, if he thought of the present, he found himself immediately overwhelmed with amazement and horror. What had become of him? Could he really be this person, incapable of movement, who had to have everything done for him, like a caged canary or a new-born baby? But most of the time His Excellency did not think about the present. He contemplated scenes, faces and situations from the life that had once been his; relived events and moments which his memory made real once more. He was not aware that he would die in a few days' time – he was always surprised when Dottor Càrito leant over him to listen to his heart-beat. His Excellency would look up at the doctor questioningly: was something wrong? He was perfectly well! He was equally surprised by the visits he received from men in dark suits – all Ministers of the Realm, court dignitaries or former politicians, come to pay their respects – who would sit at the other end of the room talking among themselves. Why didn't they ask to be announced when they arrived? Why did they just stand frowning at him, exchanging occasional words with each other but never addressing him or informing him of the reason for their visit?

But when Dottor Càrito moved away or his visitors fell silent and left the room, memory would regain the upper hand and past scenes, faces and situations would reassert themselves with all the force of reality over the world of shadows which the present had become. What a full life – His Excellency would sometimes think – what an *imposing* life he had led! Only one man in millions succeeds in having a life like the one he'd carved out for himself, starting from nothing and in the middle of nowhere – starting from Ribera, a village in southern Sicily famous only as the birthplace of Francesco Crispi. A land of tufa quarries, of bogs populated with "singing fish" (frogs); a land where, in summer, the peasants have to wait until sunset before venturing out into the fields, because the sun is so hot it can kill you . . .

From time to time, as he wandered through the past, His Excellency found himself running along the banks of the Isburo, the small stream which had played so important a part in his childhood games, accompanied by his friends – Salvatore, Vincenzo, Nicolino, Giuseppe . . . Seventy years on, he once more grasped that leaded net and bucket which, as a boy, he had used to catch the "singing fish" and the "mute fish" that lived in the muddy waters of his stream. He spent one February afternoon chasing the same eels he had chased in 1830, which reason told him could not possibly exist, but which nevertheless darted swiftly between His Excellency's fingers, just as slimy and cold as ever . . . Sitting paralysed in his bedroom, looking out at the sky of Naples, he shouted with joy as he netted an eel larger than any of the others – so large that his friends were envious; he cried with rage when Nicolino threw it back into the water out of spite; he hurled himself at the other boy, fists clenched, and grappled with him in the mud until a grown-up – perhaps one of His Excellency's family – stepped in to separate them . . .

Another time he had seen himself as a slim, graceful adolescent, his skin bronzed, his teeth white and his head full of dreams. He was sitting in the drawing room of Dottor

Vincenzo Navarro, the poet of Ribera, reading him his poetry for the first time. He read awkwardly at first, then gradually grew more confident, heated and impassioned, until Navarro, with tears in his eyes, took the sheet of paper out of his hands and embraced him.

"Cicciu," Navarro said solemnly, "you are going to become the greatest Sicilian poet of all time, and those who study and remember you a hundred years from now will also remember poor Vincenzo Navarro. A brief footnote in a large book will say of me: 'He recognised and encouraged the precocious genius of Francesco Crispi, the celebrated Sicilian and Italian bard of the nineteenth century.'"

He had relived his first love: the suspense, the racing heart, the evening assignations in the cane thickets with a full-lipped, dark-eyed girl who had made His Excellency, not yet twenty years old, believe he would lose sleep and reason for ever, even die, the day when she told him, tearfully, that her parents had promised her to another man and she had to obey . . . Still, after all those years, His Excellency trembled with passion at the sight and the touch of her, just as he had then; his old, tired heart beat quickly again, even though part of his mind knew the rest of the girl's story – she had been married, extremely young, to an accountant in Agrigento and died in childbirth a few months later, while His Excellency was studying in Palermo. What did sixty-five years matter, now that she was back in his arms again, swearing she would love no one but him, for ever? What are sixty-five years against the eternity evoked in such a promise?

Other women had played important parts in his life, but his meetings with them now, in his memory, were briefer than with his first love: just a smile, an embrace, a look, a long farewell . . . How many smiling or slightly sulky faces, how many blue, green, black or brown eyes; how many black tresses or blonde curls, how many passionate or soft, sensual lips, how many kisses afforded His Excellency some last emotion as he sat staring at the sky of Naples – a spark of passion in the twilight of his life! He met Nicoletta, the seamstress who had become a nun; Maria Teresa, the young widow of the anarchist; Meryl the flower-girl; Margherita the blonde aristocrat; Manuela the Creole, and little Antonia . . .

He found himself walking the streets of Palermo as a student, pursuing his youthful dreams of poetry, women, journalism and politics . . . He saw again his little flat in the old quarter of Naples and the window where the actress who lived in the flat across the alley used to stand in her negligée, displaying her mature charms to the young lawyer from Sicily . . . He returned to visit Mazzini in Parson's Green, and he knocked at the door of the man who made sovereigns tremble and thrones shake, who embodied so many of the anxieties and Utopian dreams of the nineteenth century, that most restless and adventurous of centuries. Nobody came to answer his knock, so he went to Cesarini's restaurant in Golden Square and ordered a plate of macaroni with meat sauce. In Lisbon he watched the seagulls for a whole hour, sitting on a mooring bollard by the ocean, reflecting on past and present and the meaning of human life which, at that moment, for the first time in his life, seemed pointless to him . . . In Paris he went into the first church he came to, and prayed. On that day – 14 January 1856 – His Excellency had in his pocket a parcel so heavy that it pulled his overcoat out of shape; a parcel which could have changed the destiny of the world . . . His Excellency then climbed a staircase, knocked on a door and shook the hand of the man who opened it.

"Felice," he said, "I made it! I've brought the detonators. Let me in, I have to talk to you."

Felice Orsini pointed at a table on which there stood six empty metal shells which would become three bombs.

"There is no time left for talking," he replied. "We've already talked too much." He took the packet of detonators from His Excellency but, before shutting the door on him, he whispered three words in his ear, which left His Excellency feeling breathless.

"It's this evening . . ."

"It's this evening," His Excellency repeated to the sky of Naples, and a shiver ran through him, now as then. "It's this evening!"

At times, as he sat with his eyes closed in his armchair in front of the window, His Excellency would hear voices calling to him. He would open his eyes and see, next to him, one of those lunatic friends of his, all dead now. Rosalino Pilo, Giuseppe Sirtori, Nino Bixio, Luigi Carlo Farini, and many others, would cluster around his chair and discuss the future of Italy as if their opinions could still alter it. Only Mazzini, his friend from his London days, would turn away ostentatiously and refuse to speak to him, because he considered him a traitor to the republican ideal. This gesture, instead of upsetting His Excellency, merely made him smile.

"The trouble with Mazzini," he would tell himself and whoever else was with him at the time, "is that he's never had to deal with any real live monarchs, and because of that he overrates both the monarchs and the monarchy as an institution."

He himself had known plenty of kings, from Ferdinand of Bourbon to Victor Emmanuel of Savoy and William of Prussia. Only the other day he'd been visited by Humbert I, the king who had died a year before at the hands of an anarchist. He'd seen him twice. On the first occasion Humbert addressed him in Piedmontese, as was the custom of Savoyard royalty when addressing courtiers and ministers. His Excellency let him talk on for a while then pointed out in Sicilian that he understood *na capazza* – not a word – of what His Majesty was saying, and that it was pointless to have united Italy if its rulers continued to express themselves like the shepherds in the mountains they came from. Humbert apologised and repeated, in Italian, what he'd already said to him in dialect.

"Unfortunately," the King joked feebly, "I can't speak to you in Sicilian, because I don't know it."

The second occasion had been on the day after the fall of the Rudiní government, when Francesco Crispi, summoned to the Quirinale to give advice, stunned Humbert I by suggesting he entrust his government to the first person he met on the street.

"It's easy to form governments in this country nowadays," His Excellency explained with his usual calm, "because nobody could possibly make a worse job of it than the Marchese di Rudiní. Any idiot could take his place."

"President . . ." the King had stammered. "How can you say that . . ."

"If Mazzini knew anything about kings and the people who surround them," His Excellency murmured, "most of all if he knew the house of Savoy the way I know it, he certainly wouldn't sacrifice the friendship of an old patriot for the dream of a Republic which just isn't feasible at the moment . . ."

His meeting with Garibaldi was identical to the one which had taken place in Genoa forty-two years previously, on the eve of the Expedition of the Thousand, in a villa on the cliffs at Quarto where "The General" had retired to reflect, and to decide on his next move. Garibaldi was walking in the park, and when His Excellency – not yet an Excellency, simply a patriot and conspirator wanted by the police forces of three or four European nations – approached him, he snapped:

"Ah, it's you. Everyone else is telling me that it would be madness to embark; that the insurrection in Palermo has already been suppressed, and that Sicily is lost. You alone urge me to take the risk. Are you mad? Or do you know something I don't; something that might persuade me that it was a venture with some hope of success, worth hazarding the lives of so many men?"

Unruffled by the General's unexpected abruptness, His Excellency listened, then replied, smiling:

"Sicily is different from the other Italian regions, General. Sicilians have their own laws, unlike those of the Bourbons or any other peoples in the world. I know for certain that if you manage to set foot on the island, victory will be yours. What concerns me far more is the dangers at sea. Our steamboats have no weapons to defend us from the frigates and other warships which the King of Naples will send to sink us."

The General took his pipe out of his mouth and fixed his blue eyes on his companion. He shook his head.

"You're not the only one with confidential information," he said.

One of Garibaldi's recent visitors had been a tall, thin, blond man who posed as the Italian correspondent on an English newspaper but was actually one of His Britannic Majesty's secret agents, very powerful and well versed in Italian affairs. What the revolutionary and the spy had talked about during nearly an hour's conversation remained a mystery, but it certainly hadn't been vague or insubstantial because, after a brief pause, Garibaldi added:

"Don't worry. If we sail, we will get to Sicily. But from the very start we will be up against the whole Neapolitan army – more than twenty thousand men, two cavalry regiments and sixty-four cannons. *That* is the obstacle."

His Excellency continued to smile.

"Once in Sicily," he said, "there is no obstacle which cannot be overcome with the help of our friends down there, who are many. If you can vouch for the sea, I'll vouch for the land."

And so the conversation ended, neither man deeming it necessary to add anything.

At times the past would materialise for His Excellency in the form of a flash of light, a sound, a smell: the crash of distant rifle fire; the shiver that ran down his spine and gave him goose-pimples when the Lombard students, bayonets in hand, had begun to storm a hill down near Calatafimi where the King of Naples' German mercenaries were entrenched. Amid the roar of gunfire and the cries of the wounded, a song had fallen and risen countless times – a song the whole of Italy was singing; an anthem that became the very symbol of the nation's struggle. It was a boisterous love song:

Oh la bella Gigogin, oh trallalarillallera
Oh la bella Gigogin, oh trallalarillallà . . .

That tune and those almost meaningless words evoked a whole world. In the clear sky of Naples His Excellency's eyes saw once more the red shirts of Garibaldi's men at Porta Termini; his nostrils widened to breathe in the miraculous air of Sicily and of that year of 1860, when Italy had only one season – spring. His Excellency's imposing life was frozen there, in that year of miracles and madmen, when the impossible finally happened: when bandits and subversives turned into heroes and dreams became reality . . . The year of *La Bella Gigogin*, symbol of Italy:

At fifteen she made love,
At sixteen she was wed,
Three months later she rues the day
Take one more step, my love.

He saw Palermo in the days of liberation. A man was running from alley to alley between the shabby houses of Albergaria, pursued by a horde of demons howling: *"U surciu, u surciu!"* (rat, or Bourbon policeman). His Excellency would have preferred not to be there to witness that stranger's suffering, but he could not get away in time. The rat was caught and executed in a flash: a knife stabbed him through the heart, another cut his throat, a stone smashed his skull open . . .

He saw the enemy troops board their ships on a sunlit day at the Marina. King Francis' Neapolitan and Bavarian troops, with their red trousers, now ripped and muddied, and their sky-blue coats, filed glumly through a crowd that spat on their uniforms, insulted them, and threw coins or even the odd stone at them, provoking no reaction. All of a sudden, however, a German officer stopped. He turned to look one of his abusers in the eye and replied proudly, in his harsh, guttural tongue which sounded like the barking of a dog:

"It wasn't you beggars who defeated us, or those other bandits the English brought to Sicily. You would never have beaten us! We were sold for thirty pieces of silver, like Our Lord before the crucifixion."

One evening, when the sky of Naples was full of black clouds and thunder rumbled over Vesuvius, His Excellency found himself back in Rome, in front of Montecitorio Palace in Piazza Colonna, on a mild spring morning five years previously. His escorts had to help him out of the carriage; he was old and, on that day, felt positively decrepit. Down in Africa a bungling and arrogant general, badly advised by his friends in Rome and despised by his own officers and troops, had suffered a defeat which, in a nation like England or France – His Excellency thought to himself – would have had little significance. It would merely have hardened the resolve of politicians and the army to regain their nation's honour on the battlefield. In Italy, everybody immediately spoke of catastrophe and of bringing the colonial adventure to a close. On the streets the people were shouting: "Troops out of Africa!"

His Excellency lifted his gaze towards the Corso where a few units of grenadiers and infantry, bayonets fixed and ready for battle, were keeping demonstrators away from the Palace. Behind the soldiers' képis he could see many raised fists, placards, and the red flags and black banners of the Socialist and Anarchist Associations. A lookout on the railings of a building across the Corso announced His Excellency's arrival: "It's Crispi! It's Crispi! Crispi's here!" and at once the crowd let fly a thick hail of coins, a burst of whistles and raspberries, and a cacophony of unruly yells:

"Criminal! Murderer! Troops out of Africa! We want our sons back! You go to Africa!"

Crispi stopped and turned his face, half-hidden by his great white moustache, towards the whistling, jeering mob. He even made a gesture with his hand as if intending to address the crowd, but a police commissioner hurried up and, bowing respectfully, whispered in his ear:

"Your Excellency, please, go into the Palace! We're risking an assassination attempt. We had a tip-off this morning, warning of a bomb." So he turned and went inside, while the guard on the door presented arms, as always.

Another disagreeable moment for His Excellency had been his meeting with the examining magistrate from Bologna, Adolfo Balestri, who had summoned the old man to his city to accuse him of embezzling large sums from the Bank of Naples. The magistrate had taken the trouble to establish links between various old newspaper stories dating from the Bank of Rome scandal and other news items, hot off the press: the two million lire given to the industrialist Perrone for the sale of ships to the Argentinian Government; the Hertz affair, and Heaven knows what else . . . Francesco Crispi listened patiently, scarcely replying to the magistrate's questions, confining himself instead to the occasional look that was somewhere between pity and irritation. The Bank, the money . . . It wasn't as if he'd kept it for himself, that Bank of Naples money they wanted to send him to gaol for now, at the age of eighty! He had used it to get his men elected and to further his politics. And Francesco Crispi's politics, as everyone knew, had only ever had one aim – to make Italy great. For the sake of that ideal, which had given meaning to his whole life, His Excellency had stolen as much money as possible, wherever he could lay his hands on it: banks, international finance deals, government licences, building contracts, even the sale of public honours. Money makes the world turn, after all, and this superior little fellow, sitting opposite him and demanding he account for every single bank transaction or front man, was a cretin if he believed that the internal and external politics of a modern nation can be managed without money or subterfuge and with honesty alone. You need a lot more than honesty. To make Italy united and great, His Excellency had been obliged to exploit money in the same way as he'd exploited everything that could be of use – the monarchy for example (he, a former Republican!), or the Mafia which, at the time of the Bourbons, had not yet acquired that name, but had given the decisive push which toppled Francis from the throne of Naples. He had made use of Freemasonry, of ballot rigging and of corruption . . . he had even tried to manipulate the Devil, otherwise known as the new doctrine of Socialism which made governments and right-thinking people throughout Europe shudder. But his experiment with the *Fasci* in Sicily had been a fiasco . . .

Every now and again His Excellency was approached by people he would rather have ignored, but could not, because they kept pestering him with embraces and whispered words of useless affection. They were his wife Lina, his daughter Giuseppina, his sons Luigi and Francesco, the journalist Paolo Morello, the Honourable Alessandro Fortis . . . His two nurses, Annetta and Pina, were the worst offenders, never leaving him in peace for a moment, turning him this way and that to clean him, pricking him with needles to inject a liquid which sent him to sleep in several minutes, changing his underwear, even presuming to feed him. When nobody else was around to hear they would cajole him:

"Just one spoonful of broth for Pina, Your Excellency . . . yum! There's a good boy! Now one for Annetta . . . yum!"

On these occasions His Excellency would revert to being a toddler of one or very little more, in his childhood home. He would sit in his wooden highchair with its fitted chamber-pot while, before him, well-known faces – his mother, sisters, cousins and aunts – alternated with the forgotten features of other relatives and neighbours. And there was always one more spoonful of baby food, one for every blessed day of the week . . .

> One for Monday's saint . . . yum!
> One for Tuesday's saint . . . yum! etc. etc.

His Excellency didn't believe he was going to die; he never had. He deluded himself that, when his time came, he would put Death to flight as he'd done with the anarchist in Rome who had shot at him twice but missed, one morning in Via Gregoriana, even though his carriage had stopped only a few yards away. For a moment His Excellency was afraid; then his fear turned to anger. He stood up and, since he did not have his revolver with him that day, threatened the scoundrel with his walking stick, swearing and cursing in dialect.

"Who are you?" he demanded. "And who is the son of a whore who sent you to kill me?" He noticed that the anarchist was trembling as he clutched his pistol in both hands and kept on aiming at him. His Excellency told him to calm down and drop the gun, and the man obeyed. He ran away, but shop-keepers and passers-by chased him and handed him over to the police.

In those last days, His Excellency would often find himself in Via Gregoriana with the anarchist. Every time he would smile at the man and say:

"Keep calm. Drop the pistol. If I don't die, you'll get a lighter sentence."

2

Palermo, 9 August 1902

At five o'clock on that Saturday afternoon in August, the whole of Palermo's high society seemed to have arranged to meet in Piazza Santa Chiara, in spite of the heat and the narrowness of the square – certainly not the most suitable place in the city for a gathering of that size. The small piazza itself, and the surrounding streets and alleyways, were filled with carriages – landaus, barouches, phaetons, sociables – and, naturally, with their horses, pawing the ground amongst clouds of flies. The congestion was such that each coachman, after taking his turn to deposit his passenger or passengers at the front door of Palazzo Puglia, had to drive back to Piazza Bologni to await their return. At the entrance to the Palazzo a liveried servant was examining invitations one by one, reading the names and titles out loud and turning each time towards a couple of disreputable-looking characters who were leaning against the wall, arms folded and apparently idle: plainclothes policemen, sent to ensure that the event did not overstep the limits of a private reception and become a public demonstration. On the instructions of his employer, Avvocato Vincenzo Puglia, the butler announced each guest to the police officers as if they had been the owners of the house.

"Cavalier Gaetano Tasca!" he announced, or "Cavalier Giuseppe Policastrelli and Signora Policastrelli! Avvocato Giardina, Mayor of Cefalú! His Excellency the Principe di Monforte! Avvocato Vincenzo di Maio! Cavalier Rodrigo

Licata di Bàucina! Avvocato Mavaro, Mayor of Lercara!" and so on. The plainclothes men looked on indifferently, as if what was going on in that house had nothing to do with them and they had merely stopped off to watch the procession of aristocrats and fashionable people. One of them, however, did have a pencil behind his ear, and from time to time would pull out a small notebook, lick the lead, and write down one of the names which the butler was still proclaiming in his grandest manner, for their benefit alone.

"The Honourable Giuseppe di Stefano and Signora di Stefano! The Honourable Giovan Battista Avellone! Avvocato Dominici Longo, Mayor of Termini Imerese! His Excellency the Conte di Monroy! The Reverend Canon Buttitta! Dottor Antonino Ferrara and Signora Ferrara! His Excellency the Principe di Resuttana! Commendator Giuseppe Pitré! Avvocato Giovanni Agnello and Signora Agnello! Avvocato Ernesto Pagano! The Reverend Monsignor Arturo Crisafi!"

When the guests passed through the half-open door they found themselves in a stone-flagged courtyard where a hundred or so people were already exchanging kisses, embraces and handshakes, gathering to talk in small circles or calling across from one group to another: "*Commendatore! Dottore!* What a pleasure to see you!"

"What a lovely gathering! What a wonderful occasion! My dear *Principe!*"

The mournful notes of a waltz drifted out from the raised ground-floor salons across the courtyard. The hum of male and female voices, the ring of glasses and the sound of laughter might have led a stranger, unaware of recent events in Palermo, to conclude that he found himself in the middle of a fashionable reception. But there was too much of a crush for a reception – there were people everywhere. Even the great staircase, which to this day opens at courtyard level into a monumental gallery to the right of the front door, was thronged with lords, ladies and gentlemen who were removing their jackets because of the heat and talking about something which had to be done that very day, as it would soon be too late.

"The way things are going, my friends," a man with a grey beard and a stentorian tone (the lawyer Collotti Catalano) proclaimed to one knot of people, "we cannot stay silent any longer. Matters have reached a head, and prudence on our part would only be mistaken for cowardice or, worse still, an admission of guilt!"

Professor Giuseppe Pitré took a few steps into the centre of the courtyard, in the direction of the salons, and saw Dottor Angelo Puglia, son of the house, making his way towards him. The doctor embraced him, kissed him on both cheeks and thanked him for coming.

"Professor . . ." he said. "What a great honour; what a great pleasure! Allow me to accompany you upstairs – the Honourable Perrone Paladini from Messina and the other people of consequence who will be addressing the meeting are all up there. Naturally we're counting on you to contribute. The words of a well-known scholar such as yourself are essential to help us recover the lost honour of our poor island, now that such disgraceful stories are being put about."

Professor Giuseppe Pitré was a man of around sixty, with grey hair and beard, and a broad forehead that reached almost to the top of his head. He nodded.

"My opinions on the Palizzolo affair and the so-called Mafia," he replied, somewhat self-importantly, "were expressed in my newspaper article several days ago, but I'd be happy to repeat them for the benefit of an audience which, I have been informed and I now see for myself, represents the cream of high society from Palermo and the whole of Sicily."

The upstairs rooms, like those on the ground floor, were crowded with important guests, and Dottor Puglia and Professor Pitré had to exchange many embraces – with Avvocato Dagnino,

Ingegner Torrente, Conte Galletto, Commendator Tesauro, the notary Signor Cavarretta and his two sons, Commendator Nocito, and others too numerous to list – before managing to reach Vincenzo Puglia, who was making his way towards the top of the staircase in the company of Commendator La Manna, Avvocato Perrone Paladini and Professor Ragusa Moleti. Their greetings were warm but brief, because the master of the house kept checking his watch anxiously.

"We simply have to start on time," he insisted. "We must hurry! We've got journalists here from all the main Sicilian and Italian papers. If we want our Committee to be mentioned in tomorrow's editions, we have to give them time to write their articles! We promised we would!"

By now the courtyard was packed solid. People were everywhere: at the windows, on the balconies, on the landings of the staircase ... When the white head and beard of the former Member of Parliament Perrone Paladini appeared at the top of the arcade, there were many cheers and an immensely long round of applause which seemed about to end at least three times, only to start up again, thunderously. When silence finally fell, the floor was taken by Commendator La Manna, who had been given the task of chairing the meeting, and was visibly moved.

"Sicilian friends and brothers!" the *commendatore* said. "On the night of the thirtieth of July, when the telegraph office conveyed from Bologna the news that the Notarbartolo trial had ended with the sentencing of the Honourable Raffaele Palizzolo to thirty years' imprisonment, we citizens of Palermo found it hard to sleep. There hovered above us the certainty that a terrible injustice had been perpetrated against a compatriot and against the whole of Sicily; that the entire population of our island had been tried and condemned on the basis of a slanderous and nonsensical prejudice. Our legal and ethical consciences were affronted by a judgment we considered iniquitous, passed by a distant and openly hostile court. For the past nine days, my Sicilian friends and brothers, this insult has been tormenting our souls and disturbing our sleep."

At this point the *commendatore* was interrupted by cries of "Hear! hear!" and "Quite right!" and a thunderous burst of applause – the first of many during the course of the meeting.

"However," the orator continued, wiping his brow with a large blue handkerchief, "we have too deep a respect for the laws which govern us to question the decision of a court. We have given our word of honour to the Prefect that the city of Palermo will behave in a mature and civilised fashion, and will refrain from expressing its contempt for the sentences passed on the defendants Palizzolo and Fontana.

"We are not gathered here," Commendator La Manna began again after a brief pause, "to protest against a sentence passed with all the superficial trappings of legality. We are gathered to deplore the attitude of those Bolognese and Italians who, by their unruly harangues against Sicily and against some supposed criminal organisation called the Mafia, poisoned the atmosphere in which the lives of many men were to be decided.

"The people of Palermo are an ancient and extremely patient race who, over the centuries, have endured many rulers and abuses of power. But they are also proud and aloof; they have kept their identity and dignity intact and will not allow anyone, Italian or foreign, to preach to them!" (Thunderous applause).

Professor Pitré came forward. "Commendator La Manna," he said, "has perfectly articulated every Palermitan's view of events in Bologna. I too feel compelled to speak up in defence of our beloved Sicily, which I trust I know better than those who condemn it without even having been here, basing their opinions purely on prejudice, tittle-tattle and myths handed down from generation to generation." (Laughter and applause).

"For many years – *far* too many years," Professor Pitré continued, warming to his subject, "the Italian press has restricted its coverage of Sicily to the celebration of its landscape or, more often, to the condemnation of the moral shortcomings of its inhabitants.

"Particularly of late, the name of Sicily is never mentioned without the word Mafia – they are considered one and the same. This pernicious process has been completed by the recent trial of Palizzolo and Fontana, which gave credence to the myth that, here in Sicily, the most atrocious crimes are carried out by a shadowy sect which reaches up to the highest echelons of the State and down into the very gutter. Its tentacles extend to the upper classes; its coils envelop men and women, young and old, rich and poor – everyone born and bred in this land of mysteries, which Nature showered with infinite gifts but man has rendered uninhabitable. No Sicilian – the Bologna judges imply with their sentence – can escape the dreadful, terrifying influence of this organisation!" (Laughter, applause and remarks).

Professor Pitré paused for a moment, as if to ponder his own words.

"This is outrageous nonsense!" he exclaimed at last, "and the soul of every good Sicilian rises in indignation against it. How can such a sinister legend have grown up around this poor island?" He gestured towards the man next to him – a more impressive figure, taller and whiter of beard. "The Honourable Perrone Paladini fought at Garibaldi's side to oust the Bourbons from the throne of Naples and will no doubt remember that – until 1861 and Sicily's unification with the rest of Italy – this secret society, so talked about today, did not exist; nor did the word that designates it – Mafia. Now, I ask myself, and I ask Perrone Paladini: who brought it here?" (Loud applause and cries of encouragement: "Well said! Hear! Hear!")

"The Piedmontese," replied Perrone Paladini, precipitating a veritable ovation, "or at least their governments." He paused to give the crowd time to express its enthusiasm. "Before 1860, we who built Italy conspired and fought for freedom and justice," he cried, "and after 1860 we had to carry on fighting – against Italian governments which did not recognise our rights then, and never have since. A government which despised and ignored us caused the revolt of 1866.

"So what is the solution?" Perrone Paladini asked. "Not a revolution, certainly," he answered, "nor separation; but some initiative has to be taken to demand, to *enforce* the respect which is due to us."

The crowd had fallen silent. Between Perrone Paladini's sentences one could hear the buzzing of the flies of the summer of 1902. The speaker, sensing the expectation in his audience, judged that the moment had come for him to articulate his proposal.

"We are, and always have been, in favour of a united Italy," he said. "We suffered and fought to make this country great, so our words are above suspicion. But some of the things which have been said and done during the Milan and Bologna trials are an intolerable affront which we must respond to, if the North is not to continue oppressing and abusing us.

"A cry of indignation," continued Perrone Paladini, raising his voice, "arose throughout Sicily as soon as the news of the verdict against Palizzolo and Fontana arrived. It was suggested – and we immediately agreed – that we should found a permanent Palermo-based committee, whose task it will be to defend our rights and our dignity – an organisation which will be known as the Pro-Sicily Committee."

These last words were drowned by several minutes of applause. Only once the clapping had subsided was Perrone Paladini able to finish.

"The Pro-Sicily Committee," he proclaimed, "will prove to the world that our island is not the land of the Mafia, and will campaign for Palizzolo and Fontana to be given a retrial: to violate the human rights of any one of us is to insult the rights of all!" He paused for breath, then continued:

"I belong to the generation which sacrificed itself for unity, so I will conclude with the cry 'Italy for ever!', but above all 'Sicily for ever!'"

The whole building erupted: "Sicily for ever! Long live Perrone Paladini! Long live Palizzolo!"

Commendator La Manna returned to the balustrade.

"Friends," he said, "may I have your attention please? Avvocato Vincenzo Puglia, our host, has asked me to tell you that he is deeply sorry to have to keep you all standing and that he apologises to each of you individually, but no building in Palermo – not even the Palazzo Reale – would have enough chairs to seat everybody here today. However, he wishes to inform you that he has arranged a buffet on the ground floor with waiters, and armchairs for those who wish to sit. Professor Ragusa Moleti will now speak a few words," he said, indicating a tall bald man in tortoiseshell glasses who was standing next to him. "Then," he went on, "we will vote on the Honourable Perrone Paladini's proposal to found a Pro-Sicily Committee for the defence of Sicilian interests in Italy and the world."

Professor Ragusa Moleti enjoyed – if that is the right word – a discreet reputation as a carrier of the Evil Eye, and many a guest's hand was plunged into a pocket and made into a partial fist, leaving the index and little finger extended to make the protective sign of "the horns".

"The Northern newspapers," he began, "have repeatedly written – as indeed has our most influential Palermo publication – that the whole of Sicily was shaken by this incident and has come close to rioting to obtain freedom for a criminal (by which they mean Palizzolo). And someone – I won't mention names – even had the effrontery to headline a front page article: 'The Mafia revolts unopposed'.

"But the Mafia," continued Professor Ragusa Moleti, "is not

a sect, either secret or public – the Mafia is a Northern Italian prejudice which did not exist before unification and was invented by our beloved compatriots as a token of their deep affection." (Laughter, whistles). "A prejudice like those which afflict the Jews or Italian émigrés in other countries . . .

"Until today," the speaker began again, as soon as the clapping and yells of approval had died down a little, "our restraint has been almost incredible; and we must continue to exercise restraint at least as long as this provocation is clothed in false legality. Restraint is necessary because those who are insulting us are doing so for a precise reason – to tempt us to step outside the confines of the law, to push us to some retaliation which would justify the famous term 'mafioso'. But we, in spite of belonging to an inferior race to that of the Northern Italians, are not so stupid as to play their game." (Laughter, applause).

"Palizzolo has never been a friend of ours," Professor Ragusa Moleti continued, after pausing to wipe the sweat from his face with a handkerchief, "and were he free now, we would certainly be among his fiercest political opponents. But we are convinced he is innocent, and we will do everything in our power to get him out of that gaol, where the real murderers of Miceli and Notarbartolo deserve to rot for ever."

"Everyone knows who killed Notarbartolo!" Avvocato Lidonni shouted from the crowd. "The late lamented, God forgive him, was a randy old goat and he had an illegitimate son who, when he was old enough, revenged his mother's honour and his own by stabbing his father to death . . . It's a well-known fact!"

"It most certainly is not . . . Don't talk heresy!" Cavalier Sgadari admonished him from the staircase, provoking assent throughout the building. "Notarbartolo was a good man. We won't allow you to tarnish his memory."

"He was killed by the Train Robbers for the sake of a few

lire," said Avvocato Agnello. "That's all we know for certain. Everything else is gossip."

Like many others who were in Casa Puglia that day, Professor Pitré had held Notarbartolo in high esteem and considered him a friend, so he found this rowdy public discussion uncomfortable. He decided that his presence was no longer required and that he could go to the buffet to get an iced drink. Little by little he managed to descend the staircase, pausing at every step to embrace dignitaries and kiss the hands of their ladies. He crossed one ground-floor room then the next and, just as he was thinking he had escaped the crush and the embraces, he saw, bearing down on him with open arms, Monsignor Paolo Favagrossa, an old primary-school friend. Don Paolo hugged him so hard it almost hurt.

"Thank you, thank you!" he breathed into Professor Pitré's face. "Thank you for sharing the emotions of those of us who felt our blood boil upon seeing our beloved Sicily insulted and trodden underfoot!"

"Thank *you* for being with us, Don Paolino," the professor replied, once he had managed to struggle free from the madman's grip. "I met many priests upstairs – I think it's an excellent sign that our clergy feel an allegiance to Sicily as well as to the Church . . ."

"But how can you say that, Peppino!" Don Paolo looked surprised, even annoyed. "You're doing us a great injustice without even realizing it. Every priest in Sicily would like to be here today, and the same goes for the monks and nuns . . . That's the truth! If we hadn't received certain directives from above, orders not to get involved . . . there would be more cassocks in this building than laymen's suits, let me tell you. Naturally the bishops have a duty to douse the fires of passion, because the Gospels teach that all men are brothers and that the same God who made Sicily made the North too, on a bad day. Still, if I had those Bologna judges in front of me now, I certainly wouldn't lift my hand to bless them . . ."

Every now and then, from the courtyard, they heard Commendator La Manna, who must have been audible even out on the street, as he raised his voice to stress the most important passages of his speech: ". . . taking up the universal refrain of our most upright and impartial citizens . . . resolve to found a permanent committee to maintain strong ties between all the towns on the island, in defence of their interests and dignity . . ."

Professor Pitré took Monsignor Favagrossa by the arm and steered him towards the buffet in the next room.

"You're perfectly right, Don Paolino," he said, "and the Sicilian people are right too – right to be fed up with the abuse and bullying. But, since it seems extremely unlikely that the Northerners will ever understand us Sicilians, I believe that if we want peaceful coexistence, *we* are the ones who will have to make an effort to understand them."

He sank into an armchair and hailed a waiter. Don Paolo seated himself opposite.

"I know these Northerners," the professor said. "They, like us, are for the most part excellent people: hard-working and devoted to their families. They consider us different chiefly because of the two emotions – friendship and honour – which we Sicilians feel more powerfully than they do. And since they find this difference rather intimidating, they've made up this fairy tale about us being mafiosi . . ."

He broke off because the waiter had arrived. Both men ordered a mint sorbet, and only some minutes later, when the large glasses had been emptied and returned to the tray, did Professor Pitré feel bound to finish what he'd been saying.

"The so-called Mafia," he explained to Don Paolino, who listened, nodding forcefully at intervals, "consists of nothing more than the rather heightened awareness Sicilians have of their personality, their honour and their dignity, which will not tolerate oppression of any kind. In those already inclined towards wrongdoing, or in the lowest levels of society, this attitude can lead to crime."

His words were drowned out by Commendator La Manna's cry of: "Sicily for ever!" which was greeted with prolonged applause – an ovation that made every window in the building rattle.

"Long live the Pro-Sicily Committee! Sicily for ever!"

"Long live *L'Ora!*" (a Palermo newspaper which, unlike the *Giornale di Sicilia,* had proclaimed Palizzolo and Fontana's innocence from the very start and believed in a Northern conspiracy against the island), "Free Palizzolo!"

"Long live Palizzolo! Down with the Bologna judges!"

"I'll be very interested to see," Professor Pitré thought out loud, "what the Northern papers write about this meeting of ours tomorrow, and whether they still dare to say that demonstrations in favour of Palizzolo are being organised by the Mafia."

3

Palermo, 31 July 1904

The steamship, draped with Pro-Sicily Committee banners, slowly approached the dock in a swirl of foam whipped up by the propellers, while passengers up in the crow's nests threw coloured pamphlets to the multitude below. The band, conducted by Maestro Salvatore Garofalo, struck up the first notes of a tune half way between the "Hymn to Garibaldi" and the "Royal March", composed for the occasion by the Maestro himself and entitled "Palizzolo's Victory". Standing at the front of the crowd on the wharf were The Swan's family: his brother Gandolfo ("Captain Trouble"), his porcine sisters, his eternal fiancée Matilde and "His Vacuity" the Duca di Villarosa accompanied by his consort, his daughters and their husbands. Behind the relatives stood photographers, journalists and the police and *carabinieri*, who were holding back thousands of Palermitans who had come to welcome and acclaim their hero, and to rejoice with him at his acquittal in the Florence trial.

Filicetta was sitting in a carriage about two hundred yards from the quay, following events through a pair of binoculars. She and Sara, her seamstress and dearest friend, had hired a coach and instructed the driver to get as near as possible to the Committee ship, but the carriage had become trapped in the crowd the moment they entered the harbour gates. It was then that, as if by magic, the little mother-of-pearl opera glasses had materialised out of Sara's bag, so that now the two friends were able to see almost everything that was going on down at the wharf. They saw the employees of the "Puleo Steam Brick Works" (who, the following day, would be mentioned in every paper in Italy), wearing straw hats adorned with pictures of Palizzolo; the girls, like everyone else, asked themselves who had sent them. They saw the delegations from town halls, working men's clubs and workers' associations, holding dozens and dozens of pennants; they saw the distinguished members of the Pro-Sicily Committee strutting down the gangway and, among them, a round, funny-looking little figure in white who turned out to be Palizzolo. ("There! It's him!" Filicetta exclaimed, and Sara immediately began to clap.) Lastly they saw the crowd sweep away the police cordon and press in around The Swan, so that when the carriages belonging to the Committee and the police reached the side of the ship, they became jammed in the throng for a few minutes, while a small and apparently lifeless white bundle – The Swan's body – was lifted by many arms into the leading carriage.

"Heavens!" exclaimed Sara, whose turn it was with the binoculars. "He's fainted. Palizzolo's fainted!"

Filicetta leant forwards quickly. "Please," she said, "let me see him!"

Then came the first explosion of joy from the crowd – wild applause, and a roar which was heard even outside the port, in the streets of new and old Palermo:

"Palizzolo! Palizzolo! Long live Palizzolo!"

The unconscious man was laid gently down on the cushions of the Pro-Sicily Committee carriage, among those members who had remained in Palermo to organise his homecoming celebrations: *Avvocato*s Puglia, Collotti and Isabella; Cavalier Saitta, the Principe di Furnari and both Tesauros – the *dottore* and the *avvocato*. By the time the procession began to move away from the ship, however, The Swan could be seen standing up in the first carriage, weeping tears of joy and blowing kisses in all directions to the cheering multitude.

"Long live Palizzolo! Long live the Florence judges! Long live justice!"

Piazza Ucciardone was so full of people that, had there been a sudden shower, not a drop would have reached the ground; but there wasn't a cloud to be seen that day – the sky was clear, as it almost always is during a Sicilian summer. The weather had been hot for more than a month – a torrid, stifling heat; a sort of fever which drew large patches of sweat on the clothes of the people who thronged the streets and squares of Palermo, shouting The Swan's name. In Via Crispi, confetti, flowers and affectionate notes were being thrown from every balcony to the hero who, like a modern Ulysses, was returning to his native island after five long years of prison and exile, and the emotion generated by this homecoming was so intense that many women, and quite a few men, were weeping uncontrollably. Every few yards The Swan's carriage was forced to stop, besieged by groups of Palermitans who wanted to kiss the hero's hand, and The Swan, also in tears, leant towards them so eagerly that he would certainly have fallen out of the carriage had Avvocato Isabella and Commendator Tesauro not been holding him by the legs and clothes. All around, the crowd continued to chant:

"Long live the innocent man! Long live Palizzolo! Long live the Pro-Sicily Committee!"

Filicetta realized she was crying when the images she saw through the lenses, perfectly clear until then, became blurred and indistinct. She returned the binoculars to Sara and leant back against the cushions.

"They've finally managed to get him acquitted and back home to Palermo," she thought. This, she felt, was a wonderful day – a memorable day for The Swan, for Sicily, and for her too, even though she was not expecting to profit from the return of her first protector, and lacked for nothing. In those five years which Palizzolo had spent in the prisons of various Italian cities, Filicetta's life had continued without disturbance or significant change, because his friends had gone on visiting her flat in Via dei Biscottari and giving her all manner of presents. But ever since the Milan trial she, like so many of her fellow islanders, had been feeling a growing anger at those stupid Northerners who lectured Sicilians about right and wrong, and presumed to try them in their northern courts, as if they were their guardians . . . What did Northerners know about Palizzolo? After his arrest Filicetta, who believed she knew him better than anyone, had realized that she felt, if not precisely affection, at least a kind of tenderness towards him. Palizzolo, the young woman reasoned, was the person who had helped her during Martial Law; the only man in the world who treated her like his mother, which indeed in a way she felt herself to be . . . He was her child – what right did those monsters have to persecute a child? So she started to read *L'Ora*, and became passionately involved in the absurd, interminable trial taking place in distant, unknown towns: Milan, Bologna, Florence . . . She felt like an active participant in the affair, which brought back memories of that other time, ten years previously, when soldiers nobody had ever seen before, wrapped up in woollen overcoats too long and too heavy for the Sicilian climate, had shot at her in front of the Town Hall of her birthplace and killed her husband. Those foreign soldiers – "Bavarians", as they were called by the common people and the elderly, who still remembered the Bourbon mercenaries – had in fact been the Milanese, Bolognese and other Northerners, who came down south to push people around in their own home and thought they could explain everything that ever happened in Sicily with the word "Mafia".

The carriages were now edging their way forwards in single file behind The Swan's coach, between two solid walls of cheering people.

"I read in the paper that Palizzolo is planning to get married," Sara said. "Do you know anything about it?"

Filicetta shook her head. "All I know is that he's been engaged for the past forty years. She's a slightly older woman called Matilde. During the Bologna trial he gave her his Monreale estate and other properties, in case the judges confiscated them . . ."

"I see . . . Well I never!" Sara laughed. "He's going to have to marry her to get his land back . . ."

"He may be marrying her for love," Filicetta said. "How can you be so sure that it's only for money? A lot of things may have happened during his five years in prison – with Matilde or any other woman. They'll have written to each other; they'll have made promises . . ."

"Go on – tell the truth," Sara teased. "Aren't you just a little bit jealous . . . ?"

"Not in the least," replied Filicetta, turning to look at her friend. "Palizzolo was hardly more than a child. If he's grown up, so much the better for him. But I don't really believe he wants to get married. It's just newspaper talk . . ."

"He's almost sixty!" said Sara.

Every wall in Palermo was covered in posters. The ones printed by *L'Ora* paid tribute to a good, just man who, after five long years of persecution, had magnanimously forgiven his tormentors. It quoted a few words from a telegram which Palizzolo had sent to the paper the moment he was released:

"My one desire is the true good of our Country, which needs peace and tranquillity. I have forgiven my enemies . . ."

The posters put up by the Pro-Sicily Committee thanked the Court and the people of Florence for having finally ensured that justice was done. (Though, to tell the truth, Palizzolo and his cronies had only been acquitted for lack of evidence. Eleven years after the crime, some of the main witnesses were dead; others, weary of traipsing round Italy, had sent the court a medical certificate. A fair number had – more or less voluntarily – retracted their testimony.)

Lastly, the posters of the Trinacria News Agency simply announced that the steamer *Malta*, hired by Palizzolo's friends with money from Pro-Sicily Committee subscriptions and from *L'Ora*, would be docking in Palermo between four and five in the afternoon on Sunday 31 July 1904.

There were also strips of coloured paper plastered almost everywhere – on walls, doors, the shutters of shops, even on the trees that lined the avenues – and printed in block capitals with the words:

"Long live Florence"; "Long live Justice"; "Long live the Florentine judges"; "Long live Palizzolo"; "Long live the innocent man" . . .

In Via Cavour the *carabinieri*, some on horseback, had forced a passage through the crowd the length of the whole street, so that the long procession of carriages was finally able to advance unhindered in a cloud of flowers, confetti and streamers drifting down from windows and balconies. In spite of its being a Sunday, all the shops were open, and their windows were decorated as if for Christmas, with paper chains and tinsel stars.

But The Swan's apotheosis had not yet reached its climax. In Piazza Verdi the crush was indescribable. On the staircase of the Teatro Massimo another band, this time from Caccamo, was playing "Palizzolo's Victory" as vigorously as its musicians' lungs and percussionists' muscles would allow. Via Maqueda, as far as the Quattro Canti, was decorated with the same arches and fairy lights which, in those days, were used to decorate the *Càssaru* (Corso Vittorio Emanuele) for the three days of Santa Rosalia's festival. There wasn't a crossroads without its own triumphal arch, no little square or open space without its own central pagoda of wood and coloured paper, no wall that did not proclaim the words which thousands were straining to shout as loud as possible while The Swan's carriage went by:

"Long live the Florentine judges!" "Long live Palizzolo!" "Sicily for ever!"

"Justice for ever!" "Long live *L'Ora*!" "Long live Scarfoglio!" (In a carriage not far from The Swan, right behind the police coaches, sat Edoardo Scarfoglio, editor of *L'Ora*, with a few of his journalists and typesetters, who were throwing their special edition to the crowd – the copies, still hot from the press, had "Palizzolo's Homecoming" splashed across the front page.)

"Down with the *Giornale di Sicilia*!"; "Long live Palizzolo!" Filicetta and Sara spotted The Swan again through their binoculars as his carriage was entering Via Maqueda. He seemed drunk – he was swaying, and was only able to stand with the help of the people next to him. His eyes were staring and glazed, and he kept repeating the same gestures, as if controlled by an invisible puppeteer. He would lift his arms, turn his head, bow down, blow kisses to left and right, bring his hands to his heart, lower his eyes and wipe away his tears with a handker-chief taken from his jacket pocket, then start the whole routine from the beginning: lifting his arms, turning his head and so on. From time to time a supernatural light would briefly transfigure The Swan, surrounding him with a sort of halo, which was in fact an optical illusion created by the magnesium flash of an amateur photographer, Avvocato Vincenzo Puglia, who had gone to sit with the coachman on the box, and was taking instant photographs of the crowd and The Swan. At each flash, the people nearest to the carriage let out a long "Ooooh! . . ." of wonder, even fear. Some would cross themselves and wait for a radiant Swan to ascend into the sky and take his place at the right hand of God the Father. Others called out: "*Lampa! Lampa!*" (He's all lit up!), but such cries remained isolated because most of the people lining the street or watching from balconies and windows over Via Maqueda kept repeating, riotously and tirelessly:

"Long live Florence! Long live the innocent man! Long live Justice!"

At the corner of Via Sant'Agostino a group of young hooligans laid siege to The Swan's coach, trying to unhitch the horses and carry the hero in triumph to his own front door. A furious scuffle broke out between these *picciotti* and the police, who eventually got the upper hand and drove the hotheads back. Via Sant'Agostino was unrecognisable: hundreds and thousands of coloured lightbulbs, hanging from dozens of arches, lent the street a magical look.

As The Swan's carriage turned into Via Sant'Agostino the police coaches, which had been behind him all the way from the port, made a surprise move and positioned themselves across the street entrance, blocking it to the rest of the procession. In the twinkling of an eye a gigantic crush was formed; a traffic-jam stretching from Piazza Verdi to Piazza Villena, in which no carriage could advance so much as an inch and even pedestrians had trouble moving more than a few steps. Filicetta and Sara, determined to see their hero again at any price, paid and tipped their coachman well, then abandoned him in the middle of the crowd. They elbowed their way across Via Maqueda and went down a deserted alleyway to Piazza degli Aragonesi, where Sara had a friend whose top-floor flat overlooked the church of San Marco and The Swan's house. From that vantage point, taking turns with the binoculars, they saw the lines of *carabinieri* and police keeping the crowds away from the front door surmounted by the Duca di Villarosa's crest. They saw The Swan descend from the Pro-Sicily Committee carriage with the help of Avvocato Isabella and Dottor Tesauro, then faint a second time into the arms of his companions. Finally they saw Palizzolo's brothers take him inside, holding him around the waist and under the arms. They heard the applause which rose from one end of the street to the other once the door shut behind The Swan, and hundreds of voices calling for a speech:

"Speech! Speech! Let Palizzolo speak!"

A man in a dark suit appeared on a second-floor balcony of The Swan's house. Using his cupped hands as a megaphone, he announced that he had something to say on Palizzolo's behalf.

"The Honourable Palizzolo," the man, Cavalier Saitta, shouted, "has been sorely tried by the exertions and emotions of these last few days, and has had to receive medical attention. But as soon as he is strong enough he will come out to express personally his joy at returning among you and to thank you for your welcome, which makes up for so many past sorrows and injustices."

After this message, Cavalier Saitta went back inside, but every face on the street remained upturned; every eye fixed on that balcony where the hero was to appear. When The Swan did finally emerge, he was being supported by his brother Gandolfo and by Avvocato Puglia. He opened his mouth to speak but, confronted with the crowd's explosion of joy, his face crumpled and he burst into tears. He covered his eyes with his left hand, waving his right two or three times to signify that he could not speak, then turned hurriedly away and disappeared, while the people below clapped their hands and chanted his name:

"Palizzolo! Palizzolo! Palizzolo!

"Palizzolo! Palizzolo! Palizzolo!

"Palizzolo! Palizzolo! Palizzolo!"

At last The Swan came back out onto the balcony, his face wet with tears. Trembling, he leant against the balustrade and, in the silence that had fallen over Via Sant'Agostino, his voice broken by sobs, spoke the following words, which were to appear a few hours later in every newspaper in Italy.

"Brother Sicilians, people of Palermo. I bless the martyrdom of two trials and five years' incarceration, since they have earned me such a display of your love! I have suffered greatly, but I have forgiven everyone. I ask those who care for me never to utter a word about a past I do not want to remember – all that interests me now is your affection. I thank you with all my heart and would be grateful if you would now disperse, because the Prefect has informed us that he will not allow speeches or other demonstrations in front of my house."

He blew his nose noisily. All eyes were now wet with tears: in the street, in the windows and even in the apartment on the third floor in Piazza degli Aragonesi, where the lady of the house and her family were sobbing, and where Filicetta and Sara had to keep dabbing their eyes with handkerchiefs so as not to mist up their binoculars. The Swan went back inside and Avvocato Isabella came out to say:

"Fellow-citizens of Palermo! On behalf of the Pro-Sicily Committee, I thank you for having responded to our invitation in such numbers, and ask you to disperse, so as not to create problems with the police. Those who wish to carry on celebrating the Honourable Palizzolo's victory can do so in his Albergaria constituency, where the gathering has been authorised by the police because it coincides with the festival of the Madonna del Carmine, the district's patron. The Honourable Palizzolo will not, of course, be with you, but there will be fireworks and two brass bands and, at midnight, as our posters announced, Signor Vincenzo Bellavia and Signor Giuseppe Dentice's aerostatic balloon will begin its ascent from Piazza Ballaro. They will attempt to reach Florence with five thousand pamphlets, conveying to that distant and noble city the greetings and thanks of the people of Palermo. Everybody to Albergaria! The celebrations continue!"

Avvocato Isabella's words were followed by one last, sustained burst of applause, then the crowd began to stream towards Via Maqueda or disperse into the alleys on the Capo side. The only people who stayed on were the *picciotti* who had tried to detach the horses from The Swan's carriage. They stood at the corner between Via Sant'Agostino and Vicolo San Marco, confronting the cordon of *carabinieri* in front of Palazzo Villarosa, and yelling at them from time to time:

"Long live the Florence judges! Long live Palizzolo! Long live Justice!"

4

Palermo, 1 August 1904

Through the gold-rimmed lenses of his spectacles The Swan was observing the hands of the man at the other end of the sofa, and the nib of his fountain pen moving swiftly over the pages of a notebook. The pen stopped, and the man lifted a face framed by a handsome grey beard. His eyes met The Swan's.

"Sir," he asked, "a few days ago, just after you were released, you announced your intention to request an audience with His Majesty the King. If it is granted, what matters do you intend to raise with him?"

Every corner of the Duca di Villarosa's drawing room, where this interview was taking place, was crammed with flowers that had been sent from all over Sicily in bunches, in armfuls, even in whole cart-loads, to celebrate the hero's acquittal and triumphant return to his beloved Sicily. The whole house was filled with flowers – especially jasmine and white lilies, symbols of innocence – and the scent was overpowering. There were bouquets in the entrance hall, on the stairs, in The Swan's rooms on the first floor and in his brothers' and sisters' apartments on the upper floors. On the other side of the drawing-room door, in the hall, one could hear the voices of guests asking after the Honourable Member ("Is he well? Is he at home? Did he sleep well last night?"), and his relatives' replies. The stream of Palermitans passing through the Palizzolo family home – interrupted shortly after twelve the previous night – had resumed on this Monday morning and showed no sign of abating; on the contrary, it was increasing steadily from hour to hour. Equally relentless was the coming and going of telegraph-boys between the central post office and Via Sant'Agostino. From time to time *Zu* Tano the doorman, or one of The Swan's porcine sisters, after knocking discreetly on the drawing-room door, would come in and place on the table – already covered with hundreds of messages – a tray piled high with recent telegrams, which the Honourable Member would read out ostentatiously to any journalists or other visitors who happened to be with him at the time.

"The Town Council of the city of Siracusa," he would proclaim, "applauds the just and wise decision of the Florentine judges . . . The people of Misilmeri . . . The whole of Ciminna regardless of party affiliations . . . The American Pro-Palizzolo Committee, Detroit branch . . . The chairman and editorial team of the weekly *Sicilia Cattolica* . . ."

"As soon as I am able go to Rome," The Swan said, "I will, as I announced, ask for an audience with His Majesty Vittorio Emanuele III and the current Prime Minister, the Honourable Giovanni Giolitti. I must assure them both that my return to politics, far from threatening public order, will serve to strengthen it, and will pose no threat to the monarchy. My devotion to the house of Savoy has never faltered, nor has my faith in our nation's unity ever been anything but firm and unshakeable . . ."

The journalist stopped taking notes and looked up in surprise:

"But that was never in doubt," he said. "Anyway, forgive me for asking, but what has the unity of Italy got to do with your position as a prisoner and a defendant in a murder trial?"

The shadow of a smile passed behind the lenses of The Swan's spectacles. He rose and started pacing up and down the room.

"As I was saying," he continued, "I intend to reaffirm my

loyalty to the monarchy and my commitment, in Sicily, to fighting every form of unrest and every separatist aspiration, including any which may arise in my name. But with His Excellency Prime Minister Giolitti I will be discussing other things as well, such as the procedure for my return to political life, and a volume of memoirs I have just begun to write, which is bound to cause a stir . . ." The journalist interrupted him.

"What will the book deal with?" he asked.

"In the first place, my trial," replied The Swan, making a gesture with both hands as if to say: "Just you wait and see what I come up with."

"Then," he added, "the Socialist plot against the Italian nation and the political struggle in Sicily . . . It'll make fascinating reading for everyone, I can promise you that! Now that my turn has come to speak, many secrets will finally be revealed, and the heads of many people who consider themselves untouchable will roll from the pedestals on which popular gullibility has placed them, into the dirt where they belong."

There was a brief silence while the gold nib moved across the paper. When The Swan's words had all been taken down, the journalist put the pen aside and looked at him, stroking his beard with his left hand – a habit he had when puzzled.

"You speak as a victor," he said, "but the judges didn't acquit you because you were proven innocent; only because, after eleven years, it was impossible to collect thorough and incontrovertible evidence against you. Your own lawyers and all the newspapers that espoused your cause have urged you to shun triumphalism, which is both out of place and offensive to the victim's family. Only this morning the Socialist paper *Avanti!* repeated its allegation that, in the Florence trial as in the previous ones, your links with known Mafia men were clearly proven . . ."

"Whoever wrote that was lying!" The Swan shouted. "I'll sue him!"

For a moment his ageing baby-face contorted with rage, and he raised his little fists as if to strike an enemy. After that most uncharacteristic display of temper, however, The Swan sat down on the sofa again, opposite his interviewer, and looked at him, shaking his head.

"I've already explained that it's all slander," he replied. "I've also told you that the conspiracy I fell victim to will be exposed in my memoirs. Did you read what Edoardo Scarfoglio wrote about my trial? No? Well, I'll tell you. Scarfoglio wrote that the 'unspeakable shower' – his very words – 'the *unspeakable shower* of blackguards in the pay of foreign powers, narks, barflies, brothel sycophants which in Italy usurps the name of Socialist Party, has ensnared Palizzolo and Sicily in the greatest frame-up of all time.' He couldn't have put it better. This is why I must talk to the King and the Honourable Giolitti – to tell them that the plot against me was actually directed at the monarchy and the unity of our nation . . . The plan was to incite this noble island and the wonderful people of Palermo – to whom I owe everything and for whom I would lay down my life – to rise up in the name of justice and defend me against the rest of Italy. But the hopes of the Socialist traitors and their foreign paymasters have been dashed. Now, at last, the time has come for me to unmask the villainous conspirators and reveal their machinations to the world!"

He lifted a hand as if about to take an oath.

"As long as I am alive," he said solemnly, "no Sicilian need hear talk of Socialism. And the influence of those renegades, those servants of foreigners whose tub-thumping speeches and repugnant publications seek to corrupt the morally and materially weakest sections of our society, will dwindle considerably in the other Italian regions too – that is a promise!"

The journalist looked at The Swan and reflected that the man was almost certainly a murderer: the Florentine court had only acquitted him because of that "almost". Yet he looked – and probably was – sincere in his belief that there was a national and international Socialist plot against Sicily, and in his amazement that such a great man as himself, such a benefactor of humanity, could end up in prison . . . He sat with his pen poised over his pad for a moment. "Perhaps," he reflected, "Sicily's troubles are caused by the immense gulf there is here between words and concrete reality – two remote and entirely unrelated worlds! Down here anyone who acts in his own interest is always right, whatever he does, while reason, which should be the focal point and guide of every human action, is condemned to lose its way in a labyrinth of sophistry, where reality and appearance, good and evil, lawful and unlawful, are so tightly entwined that they cannot be separated . . . and are seen as only abstractions in any case . . ."

"In your view," the journalist asked, "was the death of poor Notarbartolo part of this Socialist plot, or just a coincidence? After all Notarbartolo *was* murdered, there's no escaping that. During the four years and eight months you spent in prison you must have developed your own theory about who did it."

"If the police and the judges," said The Swan, rolling the tips of his moustache between the thumb and forefinger of both hands, "hadn't wasted so much time and energy persecuting honest railway employees, Members of Parliament and other upright citizens, the real criminals would probably have been in gaol years ago, and the case would be solved. Two lines of inquiry should have been followed up from the very beginning, but were neglected: that of the Thirteen-Million Lire Gang which, at the time, was notorious for robbing a number of mail trains; and that of the crime of passion. The latter would have been the more fruitful, I believe. You know what the French say: *Cherchez la femme!* Poor Notarbartolo, may he rest in peace, was much admired in his youth by the young women of good Palermo society. When he allowed himself to be drawn into marriage, he may well have had to break off a relationship that had gone a bit too far, abandoning an illegitimate child … It's a possibility. Why didn't the judges investigate the victim's past, instead of instantly embracing the so-called Mafia hypothesis? You tell me."

When his pen had stopped moving across the page, the journalist decided to change the subject. "This book of memoirs you told me about," he said, " – the one you're going to talk about with the Honourable Giolitti – did you start it in prison?"

"I started work on it a few days ago," replied The Swan. He stood up and began to pace back and forth across the drawing room. "In prison I had only two things to comfort me," he explained. "My faith in God and my poetry. I lived like a hermit: praying, studying, composing verses in Italian and translating poetry from other languages. My 'Song of Agony', written a few days before the judges' verdict, was published by the *Secolo* in Milan, the *Nazione* in Florence, and the *Ora* in Palermo. I also wrote an ode to Francesco Domenico Guerrazzi, as yet unpublished. From my window I could see the bars of the cell which had held that great Tuscan patriot and writer, and the sight gave me courage in difficult moments. I translated Goethe's Hymns and Shakespeare's Sonnets. I have many works ready for publication, but I don't plan to send them to the presses just yet, because at present I have more important matters to deal with."

As The Swan was speaking the journalist felt tempted to interrupt and ask how he could have translated Shakespeare and Goethe without knowing either English or German. It was clear from the Honourable Palizzolo's parliamentary profile that his only foreign language was French (and that only at secondary school level). Eventually, however, the interviewer decided the matter wasn't important and said nothing.

"These works I wrote in prison," The Swan continued, "are my nest-egg for my old age. These last few years I have lost everything, so I will need to work to earn a living. As long as the people of Palermo and Sicily want me to represent them in Parliament, I will serve them with all my heart and to the best of my abilities. Then, when I grow old, my writings and translations will earn me enough to maintain a poor but dignified existence."

"You talk about returning to Parliament," the journalist said, "but the Honourable Di Stefano, who took over your seat, might not agree . . ."

At the mention of the Honourable Di Stefano, Palizzolo leapt round as if bitten by a tarantula. He looked his interviewer in the eye.

"The Honourable Di Stefano," he replied, articulating each word slowly and clearly, "must resign from Parliament immediately. He should have resigned the day I was released. He must be aware that he was elected with my votes, and he is duty-bound to prove his friendship to me by undertaking, when the next elections come, to stand for a constituency outside Palermo – the city which, yesterday evening, chose to celebrate me instead of its patron saint . . . If he is a man of honour and wishes to remain my friend, he has no choice in the matter!"

"Is it true that you plan to marry?"

The Swan grimaced and shook his head.

"Such questions from a well-respected journalist like you!" he said, a note of disappointment in his voice. "Can't you see it's a private matter?"

"You were the one who brought the subject up," the bearded man countered. "My source isn't any old gossip, it's an interview you gave to a Florentine newspaper the day after your acquittal. According to that report, you expressed the wish to get married within a few months to a lady you didn't name, but who, you implied, is no longer young, lives in Palermo and is very rich – while you claim to be poor . . . Can you at least confirm what was printed?"

Palizzolo shook his head; the journalist realized he had nothing left to ask, and that he could finally leave that room and that house, where the smell of lilies and innocence was so strong that it turned his stomach.

"I kept that question for last," he confessed, almost to himself, "because I guessed you wouldn't reply. It's not important." He put away his notebook and pen and stood up. At the door, he hesitated for a moment before shaking his interviewee's outstretched hand, then thought: "It's all part of the job. Today I'm shaking hands with a murderer. Tomorrow perhaps I'll be shaking hands with a saint."

Left alone, The Swan went back to the sofa and lay down, hoping his family and guests would forget about him for a while; but Matilde came in, carrying coffee on a tray, and with her was Concettina, who kissed him on the forehead.

"There he is," said his porcine sister; "our hero, home at last with his brothers, his sisters and his fiancée. Look what they've done to him, the poor lamb! But he'll get better now we're taking care of him."

Matilde put exactly the right amount of sugar in The Swan's coffee, stirred it with a teaspoon, then brought the cup to his lips, tilting it little by little until he'd emptied it.

"There are a lot of people waiting to see you in the entrance hall," Matilde whispered to her fiancé. "Monsignor Crisafi has just arrived . . . Then there's the Principe di Resuttana, Commendator Sirena, Cavalier Pipitone, Avvocato Paladino and Heaven knows who else. Downstairs in your study there's Cavalier Gallina and Ingegner Santoro with his wife and oldest daughter. They're all hoping to be able to see you and offer their congratulations . . . Oh, and I forgot – there's another journalist, from Naples, the *Mattino*."

"For the love of God, send him away," The Swan exclaimed. "I'm not giving any more interviews! I've done too many already!" He brought his fiancée's hand to his lips and kissed it.

"Matilde, please," he said, "do me a kindness and deal with them for me – give them my regards and my apologies. I need to be alone for a while ... If they really care for me, they'll understand."

He took off his glasses, folded them, and put them in his dressing-gown pocket, then clasped his hands behind his head and, while he was still speaking, rolled his eyes upwards until only the whites showed – an art which The Swan had mastered in childhood and continued to use from time to time: on trains, at public meetings, at home, wherever, in fact, he wished to terminate a conversation that bored him. Matilde and Concettina hurried to the door but, as they were leaving, they heard him make one last request:

"Could you send *Zu* Tano up? I need him."

Alone at last, The Swan brought his eyes back to their normal position and began to reflect – something he had not had a chance to do since his release, because in Florence, Rome, Naples, and on the ship which brought him back to Palermo, he had been constantly surrounded by people ... He tried to assess his position. He had been welcomed back to Sicily like a king, surrounded by a halo of omnipotence which made the virtuous commentators of the Northern press shake with indignation and filled government officials in Palermo and Rome with unease ... The fear was that one word from him might unleash the fury of the crowds – those same crowds which, on the evening when the telegraph sets began tapping out news of his acquittal, streamed into every square of every town in Sicily chanting his name, and later carried him shoulder-high through the streets of Palermo. But The Swan was no leader of men – he was not planning to whip up the masses; more prosaically, he was wondering how to keep the people with him until he needed them again. What worried him most, now that the intoxicating feeling of power was beginning to wear off, was the longevity of his triumph. Would he still be the favourite at election time in the autumn, or would all the enthusiasm vanish like a dream after a few days? Would the Palermitans and Sicilians forget all about him? If they did, The Swan thought to himself, he would no longer count for anything, in Sicily or anywhere else. All his old friends had either emigrated, died, or turned into enemies, like Don Piddu *Facci di lignu*, his co-defendant in the Bologna and Florence trials, who used to refuse to greet him in court and spat on the floor whenever he went by. Sergio Trabia and Filippo Pesco had been killed; Francesco Vitale and Salvatore Anfossi had moved to America, Perez Rizzuto had disappeared without trace . . . The Monreale, Villabate and Altavilla Families were in enemy hands. Di Stefano, the lawyer who had taken over the Honourable Palizzolo's seat in Parliament, had announced that he was going to stand for re-election in the Palermo constituency of Albergaria which, for twenty years, had belonged to The Swan. Even the last of the faithful, Matteo Filippello, had had to be eliminated during the Florence trial because he'd been intimidating prosecution witnesses, who immediately denounced him to the authorities . . . a tragedy! The Swan himself had been obliged to give his consent from his prison cell; but at least the murder, performed by two specialists of the genre, had gone off smoothly – the *curatolo* had been found hanging from the banisters of the hotel he was staying in, a sheet wound round his neck. The papers called it suicide, because the Florence police hadn't thought it necessary to open an inquiry, and because nobody at the Hotel Borgo Allegri – whose clients were nearly all Sicilian – had seen or heard anything. Matteo Filippello, legal correspondents reported, had been unable to bear the sorrow and the shame of tainting his protector by association, and had hanged himself.

There was a knock on the door and *Zu* Tano came in, bearing a tray laden with more telegrams and visiting cards from Palermitans who had come to Via Sant'Agostino to pay homage to their hero. He set the tray down on the table and asked:

"Did Your Excellency want me for something?"

"Send someone over to Via dei Biscottari," said The Swan, "to that woman Filicetta – remember her?" He pulled a silver coin from his pocket. "You know how it is, *Zu* Tano," he said, conspiratorially, as he handed over the money. "We're men, and five years is a long time to be in prison . . . a long time to be alone! Send her a bunch of flowers – send her red roses – and let her know I'll be paying her a visit . . . tell her to expect me this evening."

EPILOGUE

(1920)

Palermo, 2 February 1920

A small, elderly man with white hair and moustache walked across the café on the ground floor of the Unione Club, heading for the reading room. He was so tiny and so round that he looked like a gnome; he wore a dark velvet tailcoat of the kind favoured by opera singers or bohemian painters, with a bow tie and a brightly-coloured waistcoat and, as he walked, he leant on a stick. Don Liborio watched him all the way across the room, then turned to Professor Paternò who was sitting at the same table and must have been about the age of the man in tails.

"Do you have any idea," Don Liborio asked, "who that fellow might be? I can't recall ever seeing him before, but I may be mistaken . . ."

Professor Paternò smiled at Avvocato Trigona and Ingegner Salvo, two elderly club members who had joined him so as to eavesdrop on his conversation with a young man from the capital, but were pretending to be preoccupied with their own thoughts and with the smoke of their cigars. This conspiratorial glance signified that the two men knew the gnome as well as the professor did, and that they were welcome to join in the conversation.

"Yes," Paternò replied to his friend, "I do know who he is and I'm glad you asked. That little man, who looks so insignificant and only attracted your attention because of his size, and the way he still dresses like somebody from the last century, has a life story worthy of being told by our Pirandello or even the great Verga. And yet a lot of youngsters like you, here in Palermo – even in this club – wouldn't be able to answer your question. Does the name Raffaele Palizzolo ring any bells?"

Don Liborio was the last male descendant of a great Sicilian family, now ruined. It was said that a great-aunt of his had died of starvation at over ninety years of age, forgotten by everybody, in a villa in Piana dei Colli which had once been one of the most splendid residences in Palermo, or indeed the whole of Sicily. But Don Liborio himself went on living like a wealthy aristocrat, in spite of his debts. He spent most of the year in Rome, or abroad, and was always very elegant: his black hair, shining with brilliantine, was parted down the middle with consummate skill; his upper lip sported a moustache so thin that it seemed to be drawn on with ink, and his neck-ties and spats were the most extraordinary articles of male apparel to be found in Palermo. He looked at the professor, and his pale blue eyes widened.

"Raffaele Palizzolo?" he repeated.

"Just as I thought," said Professor Paternò. "You don't remember the name, or perhaps you've never heard it. There's no reason why you should have. Around the turn of the century, when his name was all over the Italian papers, you were still a child living abroad, if I'm not mistaken . . ."

The young man nodded in confirmation. "I was in France," he said, "moving between Paris and my Aunt Nini's castle and, except for brief periods in Palermo or Rome, I stayed there until I was fifteen."

To tell the truth, Don Liborio's curiosity about the little man had been focused on his physical appearance, and the prospect of having to listen to his life story didn't exactly fill him with enthusiasm. But it was only eleven in the morning and one had to pass the time somehow. Sicily and Palermo, the young man told himself, were the dullest places on earth, with their gentlemen's clubs, so different from the cafés and meeting places of Paris and Rome . . .

"Who is this Raffaele Palizzolo?" he asked, fluttering his eyelids as he always did when asking a question.

"He is, or rather was, a politician," replied Professor Paternò. "A Member of Parliament for five successive governments, leader of the provincial council and head of various associations . . . A very powerful man, always on the side of whoever was in office: first Crispi, then the Marchese di Rudiní . . ."

"A man who excited comment," Avvocato Trigona ventured to add, after exchanging another look with the professor; "like his father and uncle before him. They were country people who got rich by taxing the peasants, then moved to the city and discovered patriotism: suddenly they were all conspiring against the Bourbons, all marching heroically behind Garibaldi . . . But the Palizzolo family, unlike many others, never managed to become accepted in Palermo society, since they maintained their links with the underworld. Raffaele Palizzolo and his brothers were nephews of a famous bandit, Nobile, and they've always been close to the kind of people the papers describe as mafiosi . . ."

"Ah! The papers, the papers . . ." Ingegner Salvo, who was sitting between Avvocato Trigona and Professor Paternò, grimaced. "What does mafioso mean? Who is a mafioso? The Italian language has specific words for each and every concept, and one should use them. If one is talking about a criminal, then one should say 'criminal'. If one is referring to a bandit, one should say 'bandit'. . ." He paused for a moment, cigar in hand, gazing at Trigona and shaking his head. "Believing in the Mafia," he declared sententiously, "is a form of superstition, like believing in the Evil Eye or witchcraft . . ."

"Superstition or not," Professor Paternò interrupted, "the fact remains that Palizzolo liked to surround himself with certain characters, certain men . . . who, for twenty years, let him do anything he liked in Palermo. When the banking scandal broke – in 1893, I believe – and the Marchese di Notarbartolo was killed here in Sicily, a rumour began to circulate, ever more insistently, to the effect that the actual murderer was a certain Fontana di Villabate, and that the man behind it was Palizzolo . . ."

"Ah yes; I remember," Don Liborio said. "My father spoke about that story when I was a child. He was a friend of the Notarbartolo family – he used to go hunting with Don Emanuele. My father said it was Crispi who did it, or rather Crispi's party here in Sicily . . ."

Ingegner Salvo shook his head: "A likely tale!"

"However that may be," Paternò continued, "there was a trial – in fact there were three trials. The first took place in Milan; Palizzolo and Fontana weren't in the dock, but the judges asked for leave to extend the inquiry, and they both ended up being charged. In the second trial, in Bologna, they were condemned: Palizzolo, as the instigator, got thirty years and Fontana, as the murderer, got life . . ."

"Those sentences," Avvocato Trigona said, "were influenced by an unprecedented press campaign against the South and Sicily, and they were passed in an openly hostile atmosphere. It was a legal lynching . . ."

"Never before," Ingegner Salvo said, "had the verdict of an Italian court officially recognised the existence of this secret association named Mafia, which in Sicily – and only in Sicily – is supposed to commit outrages, thefts, murders and every other kind of crime! For our tremendously civilised Northern brothers, the Palizzolo trial immediately became a pretext for expressing their ancient, deep-seated contempt for us. So we gentlemen and nobles of Sicily founded a Pro-Sicily Committee, to protect the honour and good name of our island, and to press the Government and judiciary for a more even-handed treatment of the accused . . ."

"So who did kill Notarbartolo?" asked Don Liborio.

The *ingegnere* opened his arms wide. "Who knows? The identity of the real murderers never came to light. But one thing's for certain: they were common thieves who killed their victim to get his watch and a few lire . . ."

"The third trial," Professor Paternò said, "was held in Florence, eleven years after the crime. Some of the witnesses were dead, others had lost their memory; most of them retracted their statements. Palizzolo was acquitted because of lack of evidence; Palermo welcomed him as a hero and Founding Father Of The Nation, and he was carried round the streets in triumph by a wildly enthusiastic crowd. Nobody had ever seen the like, not even at Santa Rosalia's festivals in the old days. It's from that point onwards, in my opinion, that this story becomes worthy of being told by a great writer, because Raffaele Palizzolo, who had convinced himself of his own innocence years before . . ."

"But Palizzolo *was* innocent!" Salvo insisted forcefully.

"It comes to the same thing," said Professor Paternò. "The point isn't whether he was guilty or innocent, but that, from then on, he began to believe he was a hero and to act accordingly. I met him at that period, so I can assure you he alternated between moments of relative lucidity – when he realized that, after his apotheosis, Sicily had forgotten all about him – and moments of total delirium, when he talked wildly about being re-elected to all four Palermo seats simultaneously and making as triumphant a return to politics as he had to his beloved island. He harboured the illusion that he could become a new Francesco Crispi, summoned by the King whenever vital national decisions had to be made, and believed that His Majesty, once he had appreciated his qualities as an advisor, would ask him to take over from Giolitti as Prime Minister.

"When Avvocato Di Stefano was elected in Palizzolo's old Albergaria constituency, only three months after his apotheosis, our man almost lost what little sense he had left. He refused to believe what his eyes and ears were telling him, and stammered incoherently about an international Socialist conspiracy and a book of memoirs he was planning to send to His Majesty, which would denounce Di Stefano as a traitor . . . He couldn't see that by now he was *un uomo posato*, as we say in Palermo, meaning a man who's been cast aside, and he did his utmost to win back his electorate. For years he turned up on time at every council meeting (town and provincial), every hearing of the finance courts and every board meeting of every public company, in the hope of lifting the curse which prevented him – Sicily's national hero – from reclaiming that position in the vanguard of local and national politics that was his by right; but the more he persisted, the more people ignored him. He turned into a shadow of his former self. When he stood for election again – in 1909 I think – he got no more than a few dozen votes (not even those of all his relatives) compared to almost two thousand secured by the Honourable Di Stefano. Then there was the assassination attempt, which left him at death's door . . ."

"Assassination attempt?" Avvocato Trigona made a gesture of surprise.

"Are you sure?" Ingegner Salvo asked, shaking his head. "I've never heard anything about an assassination."

"Four bullet wounds," Professor Paternò said, "and not one of them fatal. It seems he was shot by the son of a certain Filippello, one of Palizzolo's estate stewards. Filippello died in mysterious circumstances during the Florence trial, and his son, who lived in America, became convinced that his father had been murdered on Palizzolo's instructions, and came back to Italy to get his revenge – unsuccessfully, as it turned out. It happened at Monreale, on one of the victim's estates, and naturally wasn't reported to the police. When Palizzolo reappeared in Palermo after a couple of months' absence, he told the few people who bothered to inquire that he'd had to spend some time in a Roman clinic for an operation . . ."

"Ah yes," Avvocato Trigona exclaimed. "Now I remember! If I'm not mistaken, it was then that he made a pilgrimage to Lourdes to thank the Virgin for saving him from what we believed to be an illness."

Professor Paternò nodded. "That's right," he said. "He went to Lourdes and when he got back he seemed a different man. He said he had fainted in the grotto, and that he'd spoken to Our Lady, who confirmed his status as Sicily's national hero and told him how to accomplish his historic mission. His future was no longer in politics. It was in literature. He must complete the memoirs he had promised after the Florence trial; the ones which would reveal to the world the Socialist plot against the Italian nation . . ."

"Am I right in thinking," Ingegner Salvo interrupted, "that it was around this time that the whole of Palermo began calling him by his nickname – *U Cignu*, The Swan?"

Paternò smiled and shook his head. "Palizzolo had always been The Swan," he replied, "but only to his family and a few close friends. We, his classmates in secondary school, were the first to call him that, and 'The Swan' he remained for the rest of his life . . . For most people in Palermo, however, Palizzolo became *U Cignu* when he began to recite his patriotic poems in the street. I can see him now, standing in Piazza Marina at the time of the Libyan war, surrounded by a pack of urchins cheering him on and clamouring for 'the one about the conquest of Tripoli'. I can almost hear his voice reciting the section about the 'Italic host', which had the whole of Palermo in stitches for two years, until the war in Europe began:

> "Terrible, redoubtable,
> Like to the lava of Etna irresistible,
> The Italic host advances,
> Across the sands of Africa it marches
> And, with its bravery,

Of natives and infidels the knavery
O'erwhelms, and covering itself with glory
(Matter meet for song and story),
Throughout those lands once thrall to slavery
Hoist high its banner – herald of Liberty!

"These verses – justly renowned for their ugliness – are part of an 'Ode to the Victors of Tripoli' which The Swan had printed at his own expense in the spring of 1912, a few months before he was pauperised . . ."

"Now *there's* a business I never understood," said Trigona. "How did Palizzolo suddenly lose everything? He had all that land in Monreale and Villabate and his family estate in Caccamo, as well as the house in Palermo . . ."

"Palizzolo," Professor Paternò replied, "had owned nothing at all since the Bologna trial when, to avoid having his assets confiscated, he handed them over to a Signorina Matilde, to whom he'd been engaged for more than forty years. The agreement was that the two sweethearts would marry, either in prison or at the end of his sentence . . . but then, in Florence, Palizzolo was acquitted, and all inclination for matrimony deserted him. He went back to running his estates as if he owned them, and even tried to persuade Matilde to return everything to him. But she'd got the notion of marriage into her head and, one fine day, since The Swan was showing no sign of keeping his promise, she got her own back by dying on him. She didn't even allow him an hour's notice – she just gave herself a heart attack and dropped dead on the spot. At the funeral Palizzolo sobbed and wailed and made the devil of a fuss, but he didn't manage to bring his fiancée back to life. Matilde's place was taken by a brother of hers from America, who inherited everything The Swan possessed – the two estates in Monreale and Villabate, the Caccamo acres . . ."

Don Liborio raised a hand and glanced at the professor: "Look," he said. "He's coming back."

Professor Paternò, Avvocato Trigona and Ingegner Salvo all turned to look towards the reading room. In doing so, they attracted the attention of The Swan who, noticing that he was being observed, bowed to the group and walked on towards the door.

"Punctual as ever," said the professor, looking at his watch. "Every morning it's the same: first he goes to Mass, then he comes to the club to read the papers. Now he's going back to the person who looks after him – a woman called Filicetta, who owns a steam laundry in Via Maqueda. She's young enough to be his daughter. Perhaps she is . . ."

"Filicetta!" Trigona exclaimed. "Could that be the same Filicetta who used to receive her . . . let's call them clientele . . . in a flat in Via dei Biscottari, before the war? A fine woman – dark hair, and breasts this big," he added, illustrating his words with a gesture.

The professor nodded. "They live together as father and daughter – or perhaps as husband and wife, who knows, though that's a bit hard to imagine. She's a tall, strong woman, as Trigona here said, with a pair of knockers that must be around her belly-button by now, but which at the time – when they still stayed up unaided – were her biggest attraction. He, on the other hand, is . . . well, you've seen him: a man of seventy-five who still looks like a child and has been a bachelor all his life . . ."

"Perhaps they live together as mother and son," Don Liborio suggested slyly. "You find women who keep a man in that way, rather like a pet cat, to satisfy their maternal instincts . . ."

"I always thought Palizzolo seemed a bit of a fairy," said Ingegner Salvo. "Anyone who talks like that, with all those mincing gestures and exaggerated expressions, can't be normal. But tell me, Paternò – is there any truth in the rumour that he wanted to go and fight with D'Annunzio's men in Fiume last year, despite his age, and that it was this Filicetta who stopped him?"

"Yes, because of his prostate . . ." said the professor. "Otherwise," he continued, "they're both dyed in the wool nationalists. He subscribes to the *Popolo d'Italia*, the paper which supports that Mussolini who wants to resurrect the *Fasci* all over Italy. You may have noticed the sign over her shop: 'Sicilian Fasci Steam Laundry' . . ."

"But wasn't this pantomime hero of yours, this . . . Swan, supposed to dedicate his life to literature after he came back from Lourdes? Wasn't that what Our Lady advised?" Don Liborio asked. "And what about those memoirs that were going to shake the world? Why were they never heard of again – did he abandon them?"

"His memoirs . . ." Professor Paternò shook his head at Don Liborio. "His memoirs! I read them, my friend, and so did Heaven knows how many other Palermitans and Sicilians. He used to deliver them in person, then come back to collect them. We read the manuscript, because nobody ever agreed to print them without being paid in advance – and I can assure you that Palizzolo visited every single printer in Sicily, all the way over to Messina and Siracuse, but not one of them was mad enough to become his publisher. He even went to Rome – in 1916, I think it was – to hand a scrawled copy to the King, who in those days of war was constantly away at the front. Palizzolo kicked up such a fuss that he managed to get himself thrown out of the palace, in spite of having introduced himself as the last survivor of the Expedition of the Thousand . . ."

"What about those famous revelations?" Trigona interrupted. "Those sensational disclosures he had been threatening to make since his acquittal . . ."

Paternò smiled and shook his head again. "Nothing, nothing!" he said. "Garbled rubbish! Hundreds of hand-written pages with bad grammar and confused syntax, whose only conceivable use would be to support a bid for Palizzolo's posthumous beatification, should anyone decide to take on such a thankless task. It's a hagiography! And those who surrounded him, according to these memoirs, were almost as saint-like as he was. Garibaldi and Nobile the bandit, Our Lady of Lourdes and Notarbartolo, Don Piddu Fontana and Crispi, the Prefect Colmayer, Governor Codronchi, and everyone else in the book, are the epitome of virtue, rectitude, loyalty, altruism and dedication to duty . . . Garibaldi strokes the hair of a fifteen-year-old Palizzolo who is wearing the red shirt on the morning of the attack on Porta Termini and the entry of the *picciotti* into Palermo. The Madonna of Lourdes is a verbose little lady who rambles on for pages and pages on a single topic – Palizzolo. She weeps over Palizzolo's suffering, praises Palizzolo's virtues, exalts his role (past and present) in keeping Sicily united with Italy. Notarbartolo is Palizzolo's friend: wise, but rather old-fashioned and cautious; the young and fiery Palizzolo has the occasional political disagreement with him, but is fond of him nonetheless – indeed the news of Notarbartolo's death upsets him so deeply that he bursts into tears. Piddu Fontana is a Sicilian of the old school, taciturn and true to his word. Crispi is the greatest statesman of our united Italy, perhaps the world . . ."

"And his poetry?" Don Liborio asked. "Didn't this Swan of yours have anything else published after that 'Ode to the Victors of Tripoli'?"

"Odes, hymns, libretti, novels . . ." Professor Paternò said. "He turned them out by the score, both in and out of prison, but they're all unpublished: packages of handwritten papers which he has resigned himself to bequeathing to future generations, since the present one isn't interested. One of his few confidants, Dottor Puglia (son of the sadly missed Vincenzo Puglia), was telling me only last week that Palizzolo is more certain than ever that he is the national hero and bard of Sicily, but he no longer expects anything from his contemporaries: recognition will come after his death. With this in mind, he plans to donate his entire literary output – two trunkfuls – to either the National Library of Palermo or the Parliamentary Library in Rome. He has written to both head librarians, but so far there's been no response . . ."

Don Liborio yawned and looked at his watch – it was only midday! "Palizzolo . . ." he said, "Palizzolo . . . I must remember that name." Like many socialites who have no brilliance of their own and can shine only in the reflected light of others, Don Liborio never missed an opportunity to flaunt his famous acquaintances: he took a pen and notebook out of his pocket and wrote down "Raffaele Palizzolo," adding in brackets "(also known as The Swan)".

"Next week," he explained, "I'm going to meet Professor Pirandello at a friend's house in Rome. I'll talk to him about this Palizzolo; he's more than likely to remember him, because of the trials. I'll tell him the story you told me today – about his apotheosis and his disappearance. Who knows, it may serve as the inspiration for one of his extraordinary plays, or even a novel. I believe we already have the title: *U Cignu*, The Swan . . ."